On the Frontline

Two Angela Kay Austin Stories

by

Angela Kay Austin

Vanilla Heart Publishing

On the Frontline
Two Angela Kay Austin Stories
by Angela Kay Austin

Copyright 2013 Angela Kay Austin

Published by: Vanilla Heart Publishing
www.VanillaHeartBookAndAuthors.com
10121 Evergreen Way, 25-156
Everett, WA 98204 USA

ISBN-13: 978-0615895918   ISBN-10: 0615895913

10 9 8 7 6 5 4 3 2 1 First Edition

First Printing, October 2013
Printed in the United States of America

Scarlet's Tears

by

Angela Kay Austin

Dedication

Sometimes, we don't know how strong we can be until we're tested. Those tests can be hard, and we might not believe we can survive it. But, amazingly enough, with faith and determination we can and we do.

This book is dedicated to every person that has ever been faced with loss... loss that crippled them, and made them second guess the purpose for their lives.

Acknowledgements

I don't think I can type another word without acknowledging Charmaine Gordon. I bumped into Charmaine in cyberspace, and one thing led to another, and well...as they say "...the rest is history."

Scarlet's Tears, like so many of my stories, came to me in layers: church sermons, life, friends, news, etc. One day a news story about a young soldier's death made me wonder who he'd left behind, and how his loss would affect them.

Several members of my own family have supported their individual families through service in the military. We were blessed. They all returned home to us safely.

But, for so many women and men, the loss of loved ones in service to their country is a fact of life that they deal with every day.

Because Scarlet's Tears is not a typical Inspirational Romance, it's my version of inspirational love, finding a home for it was not easy. I'm incredibly grateful to Vanilla Heart Publishing for taking a chance on this story, and giving it a home!

Thank you to my mother for perfect attendance at church, and to the men of my family for being courageous and honorable.

Chapter One

One hand filled with flattened cardboard boxes, and the other with an overstuffed black garbage bag, Scarlet turned and bumped her butt against the door handle. The door flew open and she exited the back of the bank into the low light of the alley. With her foot, she slid a brick between the door and the door jam. After a quick scan of the back parking lot, she strolled toward the green dumpster. Her back to the lot, she placed the load she carried on the ground, and attempted to unlock the bolt on the trash can.

As Joshua Davis turned the key in his ignition, he saw the man dressed in black emerge from the shadows, grab her around her waist, and pull her body into his. She squirmed in protest, but not with any effort that would separate her from her captor.

"Behind you," he yelled, but he was too far away, in his car, and too late. Joshua u-turned and parked. But, by the time he reached them and ran to the door, the man had pulled her inside of the bank, and kicked the brick aside locking them in.

"This has nothing to do with you," the guy yelled through the glass door. "Take your ass back to your car, and forget everything."

Joshua searched Scarlet's face, but there was nothing. He didn't know if she was in shock or maybe...maybe she knew the guy. "I'm calling the police." He yanked at the door. It was loose, but it would not give.

The man didn't respond. He stared wildly at Joshua, and then scanned the interior of the bank. He looked trapped and scared, which made Joshua even more nervous...not for himself, but for her.

He didn't' know much about her, but she'd eaten in his restaurant almost every day...since that first day six months ago, but she never seemed to have much to say. He thought she seemed sad. Sad and alone. Joshua yelled her name through the glass, "Scarlet."

Why wasn't she struggling harder? Her brown skin darkened beneath the man's grip around her neck. She choked and coughed. The man loosened his grip, and she gasped for air, hungrily. The knife the man held at her throat pricked her skin. Joshua watched as a drop of blood beaded on her neck.

The man with the knife yelled, "Go away. Damn it. Go away."

Joshua banged on the glass. "Not without her. Let her go."

Scarlet Anderson's fingernails were short, but she dug as hard and deep as she could into her attacker's wrists and arms. He simply squeezed her neck harder. The tighter his hold the more light-headed she began to feel. And the more she could feel the tip of his knife dig into her skin. Something wet and warm rolled down her décolletage. She wasn't sure she wanted to survive...there was no reason. But, Joshua, the sweet man from the restaurant, banged furiously on the other side of the glass. He wanted her to survive.

She watched Joshua slide his phone back into his pocket. "The police are on their way. Let her go." And he kept banging on the glass. He wasn't gonna leave her.

Watching him pound on the door awakened her spirit. She stomped the guy's foot closest to her as hard as she could, then she elbowed him in the stomach. He doubled over, and she ran to the front of the bank. If she ran to the back door he and Joshua would be face to face, and that wouldn't be good. He would be one more person hurt because of her. Joshua was easily over six feet, but so was this guy, and he had about forty pounds on Joshua. She just prayed the police would be out front by the time she made it to the door.

The red and blue lights gave her more energy. She ran harder.

"Just give me the keys. I know you've got to have keys to shit in here. I don't want you," the guy yelled.

She didn't answer, she just kept running. She'd left the inside door unlocked so she could clean the glass doors. Thank god. But, the outside door was locked. She prayed the lock wouldn't stick as usual. Her breathing fogged up the glass as she twisted the latch. The lock clicked, and the door opened. She pushed at the door, and grabbed the key attached to her wrist by a green stretchy bracelet. Although she attempted, there was no time to lock it before the man reached it and her. She turned around, and pushed at the door with her back bracing against it as hard as she could. But, the man pushed harder, and she went flying forward.

Anne Arundel County police pulled into the bank's parking lot. They scrambled out of their cars with their guns drawn.

"Away from the door," one yelled.

"Hands up," yelled another.

Scarlet threw her hands in the air, and the jittery man holding the knife froze. Not from fear, but it looked like he was trying to make a decision. The look in the man's eyes told her he'd made his decision, but she didn't think it was what the police wanted. There would be no hands in the air or lying down on the ground.

Joshua rounded the corner. The man lunged at Scarlet, and so did Joshua. The police shot.

The pressure of Joshua on top of her knocked the wind out of her. The rocks and bushes pressing against her back cut through her skin. Something wet dripped through her fingers. She raised her hand. Blood. "Oh my God!"

Joshua rose from her. He took two steps back on wobbly legs, and then fell to the ground. God, the blood wasn't hers, it was his. The man she'd been ignoring for the past six months just got shot by the cops trying to help her get away from some nut with a knife.

"Are you okay?" His voice was whisper soft.

"Ma'am. Move away from him," said one of the police officers.

She stared up at the police officer. "Y'all shot him. He's bleeding."

"The paramedics are on the way."

"You shot the wrong person." She nodded at the younger white guy lying on the ground with an officer's knee in his back. "He's the psycho."

"We need to get some information from you. We need to know what happened here," stated one of the police officers.

She glanced at Joshua bleeding on the asphalt, and at the other guy cursing and screaming on the ground, then back at the police officer standing over her.

"If you have questions then ask, but he needs help. I'm staying here until the ambulance arrives."

The police officer's questions began to blur together as she focused on putting pressure on Joshua's wound, and watched the officers throw the other guy into the back of a police car. Officers wanted to take over working on Joshua's wound, but she wouldn't let them. She'd taken CPR and first aid classes.There was no way she would lose anybody else. One of the officers fell to his knees beside her, and they began to work together. It took a moment before they were in sync, but soon they had controlled the bleeding, and they were waiting for the ambulance to arrive.

"Bitch," the man snarled from the backseat before the car door slammed.

Chapter Two

Joshua opened his eyes to a hospital room filled with flowers. The silvery white hair on his mother's head twinkled as she leaned over and kissed him on the cheek. Her soft pale fingers, scented with the bouquet of the varied flowers around him, brushed across his forehead and cheeks just as they had when he was a child. She must have plucked every flower in her garden.

Tears welled in her eyes. "I thought...," she swooped her hands around the room, "We were so worried."

"Don't..." he wanted to tell her not to worry, but his throat was dry, and it hurt a little to speak.

"Shh..." She kissed his forehead. "There's plenty of time to tell us everything."

Nearby, his father hovered, but was silent. The frown lines carved in his father's forehead told him all he needed to know. He didn't know how long he'd been in the hospital, but he knew a considerable amount of time had passed based on Jayme's, his baby sister, red eyed vigil beside his bed.

What had happened? Where was Scarlet? Who was the crazy guy with the knife? He needed questions answered, and none of the people in the room could answer any of them. Well, except maybe the guy who walked into the room.

"Doctor, is everything okay?" asked his mother.

A warm smile broke across the older man's face. "Yes ma'am. Your son is a hero. He rescued a woman from an attacker, but the police didn't know what was happening. So, they shot, but he was shot in the upper part of his buttocks. Not the back...which is a very good thing. There's a lot of fatty tissue there," he chuckled.

Tears flowed from his mother and sister. His father released an audible breath.

"So, how long do you think he'll be here?" asked his sister.

"A few days for monitoring, but then he can go home. He'll be a little tender, but he'll be okay."

Scarlet had visited Joshua's hospital room the day he was admitted, and was back again today, but each day his family was there. How would they feel about the woman that was the cause of his being hospitalized? She casually strolled past his room again, but they were all there. The red head looked up from the book she was reading. Scarlet kept walking because she didn't want to intrude. She went back to the elevator, and back to the downstairs lobby. Being back in Arundel County Hospital made her stomach queasy. She didn't know how much longer she could stand to wait. If they left before 8:00 P.M., she could at least drop off the flowers she brought and say thank you.

Sipping a cup of coffee, she monitored the elevators, and kept a steady watch on the clock. 7:30 P.M. already. They were never gonna leave. It must be great to have family like that. Her family was like that, too, but she hadn't seen them for a long time.

The elevator dinged. The red head stepped out, followed by an older grey haired woman and an older slightly balding man. As they walked past her, the red head turned to her, and smiled. She smiled back.

She ran to the elevator, and made her way back to his

room. Visiting hours were almost up, and since she didn't know how long he would be in the hospital or where he lived, if she wanted to say thank you this was the only place she could until he returned to work.

Her footsteps slowed as she neared his room. Uneasiness filled her mind and a quiver rolled across her stomach. The potted plant she had in her hands looked ridiculous. It was too skimpy and not green enough. This was not the gift you give to someone who dived in front of a lunatic with a knife, and ended up shot by the police. She could run back down to the gift shop. A quick glance at her watch told her she didn't really have enough time. Maybe, she could send something to the hospital room after she left.

She sucked in her breath, shifted the plant around for another second, and then knocked on the door.

"Come...come in."

Joshua choked on the water coming through his straw. Scarlet ran to him; she sat the potted plant on the tray table at the foot of the bed, and positioned him so she could pat him on the back.

"Are you okay?" she kept patting him on the back.

"I'm fine." I didn't think I'd see you, here.

"Do you need a nurse or anything?"

"No."

She picked up the plant. "I know this isn't much, but I wanted to give it to you, and say thank you." She glanced around the room. After a moment or two, she placed the plant near a window between sunflowers and purple daisies.

"Thank you."

She walked around the room touching and sniffing flowers. "It was the least I could do. I mean with everything you did for me." She stopped moving, and glanced into his eyes. Her brown eyes shimmered. "Thank you. For everything."

17

She didn't have to thank him. For months, he'd been watching her from his store, and while she was in his store. Any chance he could, he'd make an excuse to be outside of his store when she was outside of the bank. He'd even extended his hours in the store to coincide with the time she normally showed up for dinner. Any reason to speak to her, but she never said much. Just responded coolly, and continued whatever she was doing.

"It's okay."

"No, really. You're in here because of me."

"No."

"Yes. Even if you wouldn't have gotten shot, still that lunatic..."

He finished her thought in his head...was crazy. "Who was he?"

She looked away from him, and stared out of the window. "Don't know. The cops said they thought he was just high on whatever drugs he could find, and he thought I might have a key to get into the safe deposit boxes or something."

"What? Why?"

"Trying to find something to sell for his next high, I guess. But, you don't want or need to hear all of this. I just wanted to drop by to say thank you, and that I'm really, really sorry this happened."

She turned to leave.

"Wait." He didn't want her to leave, and he didn't know how to get her to stay or come back. "Will I see you again?"

"I don't know...I..."

"I'll be here for a few more days."

Her hands twisted in circles. "I will try."

Chapter Three

"So, are you going to tell me who the woman from the other day was?" asked Jayme. Jayme was a stay at home mom, and now that his niece and nephews were all in school, she had a lot of time to spend with him. It wasn't that he didn't love his sister because he did, but she was younger than him, but most of the time, she acted as if she was his mother.

"I don't know much about her."

"Well, if my brother decides to literally throw himself in front of bullet for a woman, shouldn't I, your family, know more about her?" She pulled up a chair beside his bed, and kicked her tiny shoeless feet up onto the edge.

The entire day, Scarlet's words had haunted him, "I'll try." He wanted her to do so much more than try to see him. Every night she worked at the bank, she came to his restaurant for dinner before she cleaned. She sat at a small table in the front of the restaurant near a window. Always quiet. Always alone. Sometimes she read, but mainly she just sat and stared...at a picture of something, or someone. Once, he noticed tears in her eyes, and he'd wanted to comfort her, but why would she allow a total stranger to step into her private world.

Ignoring Jayme, he flicked through the channels searching for something to take his mind off Scarlet, off the pain in his butt, and off what chaos his store must be experiencing with him stuck in the hospital. Nothing worked.

"There's really not a lot to tell. I met her at my store. She cleans the bank next door."

Jayme's feet hit the floor, and she eased to the front of her chair. "She cleans the bank?"

"Yes."

Her eyes searched the room. "You haven't...you didn't..."

"Are you asking because she cleans or because you care about my love life?"

A tint of red flowed into his sister's cheeks. "Both."

"She works hard for a living. Not like Cyndi."

"Do you care about this woman, or is it just that she's completely different from your ex?"

"I want something different...something more." His head fell back, and he began to flip through the channels, again.

"What are you searching for?"

"I don't know. A woman that's not chasing after bonus checks, big houses, and cars. Or, at least, someone who wants more than that."

"I guess you made sure of that when you sold your software company and took a job as a manager of a restaurant."

"I needed a break from it all."

Jayme stroked his arm. "Sometimes the people we love disappoint us, and it's hard to move on."

"I've moved on. Cyndi is in my past."

Jayme's cell phone beeped. She flipped it open and read the text. "It's the kids, I've got to go." After a few quick clicks of her keyboard, she continued, "If Cyndi is completely in your past, why haven't you been on a date since your divorce?"

"I haven't wanted to date."

"You need to know what you want before you bring someone else into your life." She kissed him on the cheek. "I've got to go and pick up the kids, and cook dinner before William gets home." She paused at the door. "I'll be back tomorrow."

"You don't have to come by every day."

"I know, but I want to be here. I really do worry about you."

"You don't have to."

Scarlet raced through her accounts. She hadn't promised to definitely make it to the hospital, but she wanted to try to get there. Of course, when you have somewhere to be nothing ever goes right. Every building had more trash than normal, and one of her employees didn't show. So, what normally took her about five hours, took double that.

She raced around the highway to the hospital. Although she'd been there before she still looped around the block twice in search of the garage leading to the section of the hospital where Joshua's room was located.

Filthy and tired, she sped through the familiar hallways of the hospital toward his room. Although she moved as fast as she could without looking like an escaped convict, she still couldn't get away from her memories, her pain.

The smile that sprang to his face when she walked into his room melted away some of her anxiety. "Hi." She hadn't expected that, or the sensation of relief that washed over her when she saw it.

"Hello. You came."

"I hope it's okay."

"I'd hoped you'd come." He pointed at a chair near his bed. "Have a seat."

"Thank you." She snatched the cap she wore from her

head, and smoothed down her short curly hair. As she unclasped the buttons on her jacket, she thought twice about taking it off. Her clothes were stained with everything from coffee grounds to toilet disinfectant.

"Are you cold?" He pointed at the wall near the door. "There's the thermostat. I would change it myself..."—he pointed at the machines tying him to his bed—"...it's a little difficult."

"Oh God, no," she nearly jumped out of her skin at the thought of him moving or doing anything for her aide. "Please don't worry about me. I'm fine. You've done enough."

His normally clean shaved jaw vibrated with laughter. "It's okay. I wasn't going to get up or anything."

She flopped into the chair beside his bed. "How are you doing today?"

"If I didn't have a bullet hole in my butt, I'd be even better." He laughed, again. "Ouch, it kind of hurts when I move."

"How can you laugh when you're in here because of me?" Her head fell into her hands, and she did not want to raise it to look at him.

"Scarlet, I'm okay. And I'm in here because I'm stupid, and jumped between the police and a psycho."

She peeked through her fingers. "You're in here because you tried to help me." Her hands fell to her lap. "Why did you even try?"

He pressed a button, and the back of his bed rose, slightly. "Because you needed help."

"So, you just go around rescuing damsels in distress?"

"I've never run into one that needed to be rescued before."

"I should've been paying attention." She rested her head on the back of the chair.

"Every night, I watch you kick that brick, and unlock that trash can. Don't you have monitors inside of the bank? And why do you hold the door open like that?"

"The monitors are in a different room, and the lock to the back door of the bank seems to stick when it's cold outside, so I use the brick. I don't want to have to walk around to the front to get back inside."

"Saving a few steps is not worth your safety."

It didn't matter. "Sure." She rested her eyes for a moment.

"Scarlet are you falling asleep on me?"

"No..."

As the hours on the clocked ticked away, Joshua kept watch over Scarlet. He knew he should probably wake her, but he didn't want her to leave. Getting the nurse to go through her purse and find her license in order to get the pass for an overnight visitor didn't take any coaxing, and it was even easier to convince her to find an extra blanket for his guest. With her feet curled beneath her in the chair, the blanket covered her entire body.

At about 11:30 P.M. a twinge of guilt ran through him. What if she had a family or children? He hadn't heard a cell phone ring or beep in all of the time she'd slept in the chair beside him, but that didn't mean anything. He reached over to shake her awake. "Scarlet."

"Hmm."

"Wake up."

She shifted her position in the chair.

"Scarlet, do you have to be home?"

"No...no one at home," she mumbled.

"Hey Joshua, I brought bagels," said Jayme as she shook a noisy paper bag.

The morning sun streamed through the thin curtains covering the windows. Before he could focus on his sister, he glanced at Scarlet. He wanted to know she was still there. His night had been filled with dreams of her. "Shh, Sis." He pointed at Scarlet. "You might wake her."

"Oh, sorry. I didn't realize you had company."

But, they had already disturbed Scarlet from her sleep. She jumped to her feet. "Oh my God, what time is it? I can't believe I fell asleep."

"I tried to wake you."

She grabbed her hat. "I feel so foolish. I'm so sorry."

"Don't apologize. I enjoyed the company."

"Huh hmm." Jayme interjected.

"Sorry, Sis. Scarlet, this is my sister, Jayme."

Jayme stepped forward and extended her hand. "Nice to finally meet you."

"Nice to meet you, too." She pulled her cap down over her ears. "I'm sorry Joshua, but I've got to go."

"Will you be back?"

"Yes, but I'm not sure when. How much longer will you be here?"

"Only a few days, I guess."

"I checked with the doctor on my way in, he's going to be here through the end of the week," said Jayme.

"Tonight my accounts run really late. I won't finish until early in the morning."

He nodded at her. "That badge on your coat's collar will allow you to come in at any time, so don't worry about what time you show up."

She touched the tag.

"They have your license at the nurses' station."

"Oh, okay. I'll grab it on my way out."

"I hope you don't mind...I had the nurse take it last night after you fell asleep."

"No...I rememb...it's okay."

"Thank you for visiting."

"I'm so happy you're okay. It's hard for me to accept that you're in here because of me." She bundled her coat more around her neck. "Bye Jayme. Bye Joshua."

"I know my brother enjoyed your visit. I hope we'll see you again."

Chapter Four

"So, how are you doing this morning, Mr. Davis?" asked Nurse Tammie. She tugged gently at the inflatable tube under his butt.

"Embarrassed, but okay."

"How's Mrs. Anderson?"

"Mrs.?"

"Yes, I guess so...technically."

"You know her?"

"We all know Mrs. Anderson. It still breaks my heart."

"What?"

The nurse stopped checking machines, and scribbling in her chart. "I'm sorry. I thought you knew. I thought you two..."

"We are friends."

She placed the chart back on its holder. "Maybe she should tell you."

"Tell me what?"

Nurse Tammie hesitated for a moment, but then she spoke. "I know her because a lot of the nurses here did a collection for her after the death of her baby."

"She had a child?"

"A boy, but he died in the womb." The nurse's dark hands tightened around the footboard.

"Why was there a collection?"

"Her husband was killed in Afghanistan, and there was something holding up the medical benefits. I don't know all of the details."

"She's a widow, too?"

"Yes." The nurse had tears in her eyes as she left the room.

She didn't make it the other day, but today she had no accounts, so really there was no reason not to visit Joshua. But, Scarlet didn't want him to get the wrong idea about her visits. This was solely a mission of thanks. Gratitude for nearly getting stabbed by a drug crazed maniac who thought robbing a bank was a good idea.

This time, she didn't wear her bleach stained uniform. If someone else was there, she wouldn't feel too self-conscious. She dropped her license off at the nurses' station, and clipped her badge back to her collar.

The months that had passed hadn't lessened the pain or the memories that overtook her as walked the familiar hallways. Tears filled her eyes, and caused her contacts to wiggle. The dancing image of Joshua's sister bumped into her at his door.

"I'm sorry." Jayme grabbed her by the shoulders. "Are you okay?"

"Yes, these darn contacts." She rubbed her eyes for the added affect. "Where is the bathroom?"

"Let me help you." Jayme guided her to the bathroom. Where she stayed until every tear had fallen, and her cheeks didn't look so maroon. When she walked out, she thought Jayme would still be there, but she wasn't.

"I'm sorry. Did I run your sister away?"

"No, she's been here all morning. She had to go grab her kids, and pick up some take out...I think."

"She probably thinks I'm crazy."

"No, but she thinks you should wear glasses," he laughed.

She laughed, too. "Maybe."

"I'm glad you came to visit me, but you don't have to. I'll be out of here soon, and you know where I work."

His words stung a little. She stopped dabbing at her eyes with the paper towel she held. "I thought you wanted me to come by. You don't want me to visit anymore?"

"No. That's not what I meant. I...it must be hard for you to visit. You've got clients that need you."

"You're concerned about my business?"

"Yes, I know my store must be crazy by now."

"Yeah, I was there the other day...it seemed a bit chaotic." She sat in the chair she'd slept in the other night. "Joshua, is that the only reason you're telling me not to return? If I'm intruding, please tell me."

"Intruding? No." He sat up straighter in his bed. His hands reached toward her, but then dropped back to his bed.

"Then what?" This man got shot for her, and now he was telling her not to come and visit.

"I enjoy your company, but I...I know it must be hard for you to visit me, here."

She bounced from her seat. "To visit you, here."

"Yes..."

"How do you know how hard it is or isn't for me to do anything?" She paced back and forth at the foot of the bed. "How do you know anything?"

"I'm sorry Scarlet. I wasn't trying to intrude on your life, but one of the nurses shared what happened with me."

"What? Who? They had no right."

"I'm sorry. I kept prying. Kept asking questions."

"Yes, you do. You won't stop. That's why you have a bullet wound. Why won't you just stop? Everything." She screamed as she raced out of the room, and back to the garage away from Joshua, the hospital, and her loss.

Chapter Five

Scarlet looped around the bank's lot making notes of the licenses of the parked cars. A new practice since her attack. Her nightly spot check of the parking lots eased her just a little. The car in the bank's lot wasn't one she'd noted in the last few days, but as she pulled up at the other end of the lot and parked, she recognized the tall red head that exited the other car.

The heels of her boots tapped out a faint beat as she closed the distance between them. "My brother would kill me if he knew I was here, but I think I could out run him right now."

"Jayme, why are you here?"

She glanced over her shoulder at the man in the car. "My husband tried to talk me out of coming, but I'm here to ask you to consider visiting my brother again."

"Why?" She lugged her backpack vacuum out of the trunk of her car and propped it up against the trunk. "You and your family shouldn't want me anywhere near him. I'm the reason he's hurt in the first place."

"No. You're not. The maniac that attacked you is."

"You and Joshua are a lot alike, but it's not true." She rummaged around in the trunk for tissue and paper towels. "If he wouldn't have been trying to help me, he wouldn't be hurt. Everything I care for or that cares for me ends up hurt."

"Do you really believe that?"

She threw the duffle bag containing the vacuum over her shoulder, reloaded her hands and walked toward the bank's door. "Yes."

Jayme hustled up beside her, and grabbed the load from her hands. "You shouldn't because it's not true. I don't know what happened. My brother told me he chased you away, but not why or how."

"If he didn't tell you what happened, then why are you here?"

"Because I haven't seen my brother smile the way he does when he thinks about you for a long time. He doesn't talk much about anything—not since his divorce, but I can tell when you are on his mind."

Scarlet paused at the bank's door. "Maybe you should know me better. You might not want your brother to be anywhere near me."

"My brother is a good man, and if he wants to spend time with you...that's good enough for me."

"Wait here. I need to go inside and turn the alarms off." When she returned to the door, Jayme stood with her hands filled with toilet tissue and paper towels. The pleading in her eyes and hope on her face filled Scarlet with shame. "I'll visit him tomorrow morning."

Scarlet nodded and waved at the nurses that waved at her. She didn't remember all of their faces, but she knew they were part of the group of people that had helped her when she needed it. The smells of the hospital didn't make her nauseas, this time. But, as she neared Joshua's room she did feel something else—nervous. She'd run from and yelled at him the last time she was here.

At the door to his room, she paused. He walked out of

the bathroom, and saw her standing in the doorway.

"Are you going to come in?"

She smiled. "I was thinking about it."

He hobbled back to his bed pushing the pole holding his IV. "Well, come on in when you're ready." He grabbed the back of his gown. "Don't peek."

"Do you find humor in everything?" she asked as she walked into the room.

"No, but I try to."

"Life isn't always so funny."

"I know. And that gives you even more reason to laugh when you can."

She helped him get back into bed, and covered him with the thin blankets and sheets. "Do you need more covers?" She wrapped her arms around herself, and rubbed her hands up and down her arms. "It's a little nippy in here."

"No, I'm fine, but..."—he pointed at a blanket on the sill of the window—"...grab that blanket or turn up the thermostat."

"I don't want to roast you."

"Did you come here to check on the temperature of my room?"

She sat in a nearby chair. "No."

"I'm glad you're here, but the last time I saw you...you ran out screaming."

"I know. I'm sorry about that." He reached for her hand. The feel of her hand in his calmed her, and allowed her to continue talking. "I didn't mean to react like that."

"I wasn't trying to pry. I was concerned."

His pale fingers caressed her dark skin. She slid her chair closer, and returned her hands to his.

"I haven't talked about my husband or my son to anyone since their deaths."

The sound of the bed rising paused her words.

"If you're not comfortable talking about it, then you don't have to."

"No, it's okay. I want you to understand."

"Anytime you're ready we can talk about it."

She removed her hands from his, and hid her face in them for a moment. Then she stared into his beautiful green eyes, and knew she wanted to share what had happened with this man, but she wasn't sure if she could. Unlike his sister's fiery red locks, he had curly brown hair. And she couldn't resist poking through his matted curls. Each silky strand had a mind of its own.

"I know. I know. I need a haircut."

"No, you look perfect. It's just I've wanted to do that for a while."

His smile lightened her heart. But, tears fell anyway. Tears she'd only shed in private. Tears that mourned the loss of her husband and her son.

"Scarlet..."

If she didn't talk now, she might not. "Joshua, my husband was killed in Afghanistan. A bomber attacked them on the road. There were two other men and one woman with Stephen. There were no survivors. When I was told the news, I began having contractions." What she described, she'd dreamt over and over for months. In her dreams she was in the transport with her husband. She warned him, and everyone survived. Then the dream would jump forward, and they'd be in a nursery with blue walls filled with drawings of letters of the alphabet.

He squeezed her hands gently in his. Her brown skin looked slightly green to her. "Are you okay?"

His touch and his words brought her focus back to him.

"It's hard to think of them."

"But, you should remember them."

"I know. My mother says the same thing, but it was easier to push their memories and anything that reminded me of them as far away as I could."

"It's hard to face loss, we all deal with it differently, but the point is to deal."

"I haven't done very much dealing with anything for a while."

"So, this is where they brought you when you had your contractions?"

"Yes, but there was nothing they could do. I was so early in my pregnancy." She fell back into the chair, and sobbed, quietly. "Everything was such a mess. My husband was gone. My son was gone, and there was no way to pay for everything because of a mix-up with benefits because we hadn't been married long. And the new insurance and benefits paperwork were all confused."

Joshua tried to get up from his bed, but she stopped him.

"No Joshua, please. Stay in bed. I'm okay." She pulled her chair closer to him, and rested her head on the back of the chair.

"You seem tired. We can talk about this later. I didn't want you to think I was some insensitive jerk. I didn't mean to overstep."

She raised her head to stare into his eyes. "You didn't." She rested her head again, and closed her eyes briefly before she continued. "I know you've had loss of your own."

"Not the same type of loss, but I divorced a while ago."

She sat up, and wiped away her tears. "Why?"

"Because it wasn't me she wanted. Just the things I could give her."

"How long were you married?"

"Two years."

"Did you want children or anything?"

"I did, and she told me she did, but after we were married she said she wanted to wait a few years."

His loss broke her heart. His ex might have hurt him, but she was sure she hadn't landed him in the hospital with a bullet hole in his butt. "Joshua, you are such a nice guy. And I've caused you nothing but pain."

"Not really. I couldn't wait for you to walk into my restaurant every day, and when you did...that brought me a lot of joy."

"Be serious. You've been shot and hospitalized because of me."

"Well, if you see it that way...although I don't, then you owe me, right?"

"Owe you?"

"Yep, a favor...a request."

"Like what?"

His mischievous smile broadened. "A date. Don't you think it's time we both start living our lives again? Maybe we could give it a try with each other."

The feeling that ran through her tickled her heart. "One step at a time. A date. Yes."

A year later...
Chapter Six

"Mom...where is Daddy? Are Stephen's parents here, yet?" asked Scarlet.

"Honey, your Dad's with Joshua..." Her mother placed her tiny hands on Scarlet's shoulders. "Calm down. It's okay." She was petite, but her mother was even tinier. "Pauline and Marvin are seated up front. I'll go and grab my seat beside them as soon as I leave here."

"Mom, do you think they're okay with this?"

"Baby, they love you as much as your father and I do. When you lost Stephen, we all lost Stephen."

Her mother's words comforted and pained her. In such a short time, her life was changing drastically. Marrying Joshua was the right thing to do because she loved him, but she didn't want to cut out her in-laws because she loved them, too.

Scarlet swooped up the train of fabric behind her, and dropped into a nearby chair. The past weeks had exhausted her, but as happy as she was...her heart was still heavy. "Do you think I asked too much of Joshua to invite them to our wedding? To have Papa Marvin...he never complained."

"Joshua's a strong man. He's been patient and from what I've seen of him...he loves you with all of the love God can give a man for a woman."

"It's scary. I never thought I'd feel this way about another man."

Her mother rested her hip against the chair Scarlet sat in, and plucked at Scarlet's freshly highlighted curls. "I know. I prayed every day for you. For us as a family. Baby, I had faith, but I didn't know how long it would take for me to get my daughter back." Tears welled in her mother's eyes.

She was sure her own tears were destroying her make-up. But, she knew she'd scared her parents because she's scared herself, and hearing it broke her heart all over again. She stood. "Mom, I'm sorry. I never told you how sorry I was for disappearing on you and the family. I just needed that time to heal. And then, I was blessed with Joshua who wouldn't let me hide from myself or anyone else."

Her mother laughed. "Especially not him."

"Mom, can I be blessed to find true love twice?"

"Baby, it happened, so my answer is, yes."

"That's not something you read about in the story books." Scarlet walked back toward the old cherry oak vanity nestled in a corner of her changing room.

"Well, baby, I believe we all have soul mates...someone God's chosen for us, but I do think that those soul mates can be different people at different times in our lives. I believe you were meant to be my daughter." Her mother kissed the top of her head as she watched her re-apply her eye make-up. "I know I was meant to love your father. And I think you were meant to love this man, and have a family with him."

Scarlet's mascara wand slipped from her hand. She jumped back in her chair toppling it, and fell to the floor...bumping her mother to the ground, too. "Sorry, mom." She went to aide her mother. "Did I hurt you?"

Her mother slid her hands down her dress as she stood. "No baby, I'm fine."

Scarlet walked back to the mirror and did a slow twirl. The lacey fabric of her dress was still pristine. "Thank goodness."

"Baby, you know Joshua is patient man, but he wants a family with you."

"Mom, I don't want to talk about this today." She turned to face her mother. "Today is my wedding day."

"Yes, baby, not today. But, you will have to talk with somebody soon."

As the doors opened, Joshua's breath caught in his throat. He didn't know how long it would take her to reach him on the dais, but whatever it was it was too long. His best man and closest friend, Pete Michaels, elbowed him in the side.

"Told you she wouldn't run out of the church screaming," whispered Pete.

"She's not here, yet."

It took months to get her to say yes to his proposal. Not because she didn't love him, but because she felt she was betraying the memory of her first husband and her baby. Counseling with his pastor helped her to see it was okay to hold on to the love she had for her first husband and love him. And it helped him to wait on the woman he loved, and get past the hurt of having loved a woman who thought the size of your bank account was the only criteria for love.

When she reached the dais, the music softened 'til the only thing anyone heard were the breaths of the people seated in the pews. The scent of the lilies she held perfumed the air around them as she handed them to her maid-of-honor.

The pastor began. "Dearly beloved, we are gathered together here..."

He missed most of it because he waited for his cue to begin his vows. The pastor asked, "Who gives this woman to be married to this man?"

Her father and Stephen's father spoke. "We do."

Tears streamed down Scarlet's face as the simple words

settled on the room.

His pastor began again. "Scarlet and Joshua have written their own vows."

Joshua's fingers trembled as he held her hand in his. "Scarlet, I think I've loved you since the moment you first walked into my restaurant. The day I thought I would lose you was the day, I knew how much you meant to me. Every day, I am thankful that God brought you into my life." He chose a scripture that he believed would describe his devotion and love. "Two are better than one: because they have a good reward for their labour. For if they fall, the one will lift up his fellow; but woe to him that is alone when he falleth for he hath not another to help him up. Again, if two lie together, then they have heat; but how can one be warm alone? And if one prevails against him, two shall withstand him; and a threefold cord is not quickly broken."

He slipped a simple gold band onto her finger.

Scarlet spoke. "Joshua, you are one of the most patient men I know. Your kindness and love helped me to heal. To learn to love again. There is no fear in love; but perfect love casteth out fear; because fear hath torment. He that feareth is not made perfect in love."

The scripture she chose told him that she was no longer afraid to love him.

She slipped a matching gold band onto his finger.

His Pastor joined their hands. "Those whom God hath joined together let no man put asunder." The Pastor's eyes twinkled with joy. "You may now kiss your bride."

Now, he could kiss his wife. And he did.

Chapter Seven

"Josh, how many times have we had this conversation?" Scarlet kept stirring the stew bubbling in her crock pot. "I want children, but can't we wait for a little while longer?"

"I'm not saying I want us to begin tonight, but baby, you've got to understand how important it is to me to have a family with you."

She spun around in their tiny kitchen to find herself face to chest with her husband. "I know, but we've got plenty of time to think about beginning a family."

He reached over her head to lift the pot off the stew, and spear a piece of lamb with a fork. "Yes, we do, but I want to make sure you feel it in your heart."

She stretched up onto her tiptoes, and circled her arms around his neck. Gazing into his green eyes, it was hard to resist anything he asked. "I do. I don't think there is anything more I'd love than to be the mother of your children...other than being your wife." She kissed him, and went back to her stew before he kept talking, and she actually gave in. They'd only been married for a few months. What was wrong with taking a little time to simply be husband and wife? "We will know when it's time."

"Yes, but not if you fight against it." He grabbed his keys. "I'll be working late tonight. But, I think we do need to talk more about this?"

"Okay." She'd pledged herself to him. When they married, she knew he wanted a family, and she thought she could give him one, but the idea of another pregnancy... God, I have seen a lot, death and unimaginable loss, but I know you are with me, us.

"Pastor Reynolds, am I a bad wife? I love my husband, but I'm afraid." Scarlet's tears streamed down her cheeks dripping like glittery diamonds onto her black skirt.

Pastor Reynolds reached over to her, and took her hands into his. Her tears rolled across of his bronzed skin. Although the pastor's office was spacious, they sat in small leather chairs near a window. The light that shone through the window reflected off the tears splattering onto their hands. "Scarlet, in your prayers, do you tell God your fears?"

"Yes, but I'm still afraid."

"But why are you afraid? God is always with you in times of trouble."

"I know, but I feel stuck in my grief and fear. So many people think I should be 'over it' by now."

"What does getting over the death of Stephen and the loss of Stephen Jr. mean to you?"

"I don't know." She humped her shoulders up and let them fall. "Forgetting."

"It should not mean forgetting. It should not mean going back to the way things were before they were a part of your life, or pretending it didn't happen. But, it should mean living."

"I feel like I am living." She stared up into Pastor Reynolds' brown eyes. "Pastor, I love Josh so much, and to have a family with him would be incredible, but what if something happens again? What if it's me?"

"From our conversations, I know your doctors didn't say

that. It was stress. Not you. And you can't continue to blame yourself for what happened. You must let yourself heal."

"I try to feel as you say, but everything I've loved I've lost."

"Last time we met, I asked you if you talk to Josh, your parents, or friends. Have you shared your feelings with them?"

"I try, but how many times can I hear someone say, I'm sorry, or what can I do to help? None of them lost anyone in the war, except for Stephen's parents, or miscarried. How can they understand?"

"They may not understand, but they love you, and they can listen. There is nothing wrong with mourning the loss of your loved ones, but do you think they would want you to stop living? Don't be troubled. Trust in God. He will wipe away every tear from your eye."

Six months later...

Scarlet raked her fingers through her hair as she walked out of the bathroom. It was much longer than it was when she first met Josh. Then, she didn't want to worry about anything, let alone deal with doing her hair every day. But, after they married one of the first things Josh asked her to do was sell her cleaning company. Neither of them felt it was safe enough. Now, her hair fell to her shoulders. She pulled it up, and twisted it into a bun on top of her head. Snuggled comfortably in her robe, she sat at the foot of their bed where Josh was stretched out reading over a contract. Since she'd given up her business, he'd decided he should probably consider doing what he does best, third-party software management. Helping small businesses streamline some of their departments: payroll, human resources, and purchasing.

"Josh."

He glanced up from his contract.

"Can you take a break...can we talk?"

He placed the contract he reviewed on the bed next to him. "I'm listening."

"I love you. You know that, right?"

"Of course, baby."

The words formed in her head, but saying them took even

more effort than she thought it would. "I want us to begin to work on our family, but I want you to know why I was hesitant."

"Baby..."

He leaned in and reached for her. She crawled across the bed, and curled up beside him. His arms around her felt strong and reassuring. "When Stephen and I met, it was one of those 'love at first sight' things. I knew I would marry him." She rested her head on his shoulder. "He'd served for three tours, and was going to retire because we wanted to start a family. He was going to come home...right around the time of the expected due date for our son."

Joshua's hand slid up and down her arm, giving her the strength to continue.

"I've never believed in fairy tales, but I felt blessed to have met and loved him. And to have carried his child. When they showed up at my house to tell me of his death and the contractions began, I felt the opposite. I thought, why give me so much happiness and joy to only take it all away from me." The anger she usually felt when she thought about Stephen's death and the loss of their son did not wash over her. She waited, but it did not come. She wasn't sure why, but it just didn't.

Josh kissed her on the top of her head.

She sat up and stared in her husband's tender eyes. He waited patiently for her to continue. "In an instant, everything changed. Everything. The whole world looked and tasted different. Stephen and the baby became these invisible forces that were always with me. Every time I felt joy...I felt guilty because they weren't physically here to share it with me, so I stopped letting myself feel anything. I shut myself off, and only when you were brought into it did I open my eyes and my heart to the world again. Thank you for being the man that you are."

At the touch of her husband's lips to hers, tears fell.

Nine months later...
Chapter Eight

Scarlet waddled through the mall with her mother. Each had their hands filled with precious treasures. Although she'd had the largest baby shower anyone could imagine. Her mother still managed to talk her into buying other necessities for the baby. Those necessities were adding up quickly, but her mom wouldn't let her pay for anything.

They reached the food court to find it crowded as usual. Maybe because she was the size of a truck, but the walkways seemed smaller. Overstuffed with people handing out samples, women pushing baby strollers, and anything to keep the attention of anyone under twenty-one. Aside from everyone wanting to touch her belly, there was one thing she loved about being pregnant. People were always nice to her. Before she and her mother could even begin their table search one was offered to them. They thanked the young man, pushed all of their bags underneath the table, and sat.

She rubbed her hand in small circles on her stomach, and yawned. "Mom. I think we should head back home."

Her mom pointed to a store on the second level of the mall. The thought of moving again exhausted her. "There are some wonderful outfits for the baby in that store on the corner."

Something warm ran down her leg, and she shuffled in

her seat. "Mom..." she watched the stain soil her maternity jeans.

"You don't have to walk with me." Her mom began to stand. "I'll run up and be back before you know it."

"Mom..." The longer she sat, the more the dampness spread. She moved to stand, so she could grab he bags.

"I promise two seconds." Her mom stood and turned to leave.

"Mom...wait. I...think my water broke."

"Oh my God! Oh my God!" Her mom returned to the table, and examined the floor beneath it. Her mom fished around in her purse for something. "Oh my God. We need to call everyone."

A sharp pain knocked the wind out of her. "Mom, can you get security."

"Oh, yes. Yes." The other people in the food court began to notice the activity at their table. "Security. Security." No one was in sight.

The other mall shoppers helped her mother flag down security, and a few of the mothers volunteered their teenage sons to help with the bags as security helped them to their car.

An hour later, Scarlet was safely resting in her room at the hospital surrounded by everyone. Her parents. Stephen's parents. Josh's parents. Jayme, her husband, and their children. And Josh. No one seemed particularly worried or nervous, but her.

Josh lifted her hand to his mouth and kissed it. "You okay?"

"Yes, but how long...has the doctor said anything?"

Josh stood. "I'll go and check with the doctor."

Her mom, Jayme, and Mama Anderson began to swap

baby stories.

"When we were having children..."—her mom waved her finger back and forth between herself and Mama Anderson—"...we didn't have such nice private rooms."

"When I gave birth to my two, they would only hold you in your room until it was time to actually have your baby, and then they'd wheel you to a birthing room," said Jayme.

"It's amazing that now they do it all in one room," added Mama Anderson.

Josh returned with the doctor who checked her cervix and the monitors attached to her, and then declared, "I'm sorry Mrs. Davis, but I think you still have quite some time, yet."

"Really?"

"The nurse and I will continue to check in on you. And if this goes later than expected, and I'm not here...they have my numbers. They will be able to reach me, and I'll be back before you know it."

Fourteen hours later, with an epidural in her back, too many pillows, and a bed that she just couldn't seem to find a comfortable position in, she was hot, sweaty and pushing at the coaching of her doctor.

With Josh by her side, she pushed, puffed, and prayed. God, please protect my child.

"One more time," said her doctor.

She couldn't feel anything. But, she pushed as hard as she could, her doctor smiled at her, and said, "She's here."

Machines beeped, fabric rustled, metal scraped, but her baby didn't make a sound. Shouldn't she be crying?

Her heart stopped as she watched the doctor hand her child to a nearby nurse. The nurse stepped away to a table, and did something to her baby's mouth, and then she heard it, her baby's cry. The sound made her cry. She looked at Josh, and he was crying.

"I love you," he said.

"Thank God because I love you with all of my heart."

After a few more moments, the nurse returned with her baby bundled in a blanket, and handed the tiny package to Scarlet.

"Hello...I'm your mom and this is your daddy, Josh."

A gurgle was the only response.

Everything after that was a blur. The doctor said something about afterbirth. There was stitching. Something cold and soothing. And then, she was told that both she and her baby had fevers. They both needed to stay for a few days.

Two days later, her fever was gone, and she was released from the hospital. Her baby, Stephanie Davis, wasn't.

At 10:00 in the morning Scarlet walked out of the hospital. By noon, she had researched every website she could find in order to know more about the disease, jaundice, which held their daughter prisoner in the hospital. Not again. This could not happen to one woman twice. The first time she did not get the chance to know her son, but this time she actually held her daughter in her arms and she knew God would not let that memory burn in her mind and her heart for the rest of her life.

As she clicked the keyboard to go to yet another site she found that everything her doctor told her was true, but it didn't make her feel any more comfortable.

Josh walked into the computer room and pulled up a chair beside her. He grabbed her hands, and wrenched them away from the keyboard. "Baby, the doctor told us this was common. This is 'normal' jaundice. We should feel blessed it's not something more severe."

"But...what if the phototherapy doesn't work? What if her little liver can't push all of the gunk out? This disease could cause all kinds of things: cerebral palsy and deafness."

"Baby, you're forgetting that we're not alone in this. God is with us. He will not leave us, although we're in a dark place, I can't believe he brought us this far to leave us."

"Then why? Why do we have to go through this?"

"I don't know; but, I do know that when we have our baby home, we will love her like no one has ever loved their child. Because we'll know the pain of not coming home with our child and understand the loss of a child. God is close to us because of our broken hearts. And I believe he'll bless us because he knows our hearts and spirits. Don't you believe, too?"

She squeezed her husband's hands. "God is my strength, and so are you."

Epilogue

Psalms 73:26 *My flesh and my heart faileth: but God is the strength of my heart and my portion forever.*

Seeing their daughter underneath that light in the neonatal unit pained Scarlet and that broke Joshua's heart. He knew that for Scarlet, the only thing that would have been perfect was perfection. To have birthed their baby girl, and walked out of the hospital a day later with barely a thought that they were there. Their pictures and their new baby would have been the only memories.

If he were completely honest with himself, the same would be true for him, too. He'd prayed so hard over the last nine months. Asking God to watch over his wife and his child because he didn't know how much more loss she could take and he knew he could not take losing her.

He would prefer to be awakened for 3:00 A.M. feedings instead of to the silent sobs of his wife. But because he'd never lost a child his wife had fears he was challenged to console. Fears he didn't have...until the doctor told them Stephanie's symptoms had escalated into a more severe case. But, he prayed and knew everything would go as God intended. He prayed God's plan allowed them to bring their daughter home.

Night after night, he watched his wife cry herself to sleep. He saw her leave uneaten food on her plate, and ignore phone calls from concerned family. He'd only just been given his wife. To lose her again would cause him to possibly lose himself.

Although she cried after each trip to the hospital, she visited their daughter every day. Today was no different than the previous. Their daughter's tiny yellow-tinted frame lie beneath the lights intended to help her body rid itself of the build-up of toxins making her sick. Toxins overwhelming her liver.

Stephanie opened her eyes, and they were green...just like his, but their yellow tint stabbed him in his heart. At their sight, Scarlet's tears began to trickle down her cheeks. The tighter he held her, the more determined she seemed to be not to let them fall.

"She will be okay," he whispered.

"I pray." She glanced into his eyes briefly. "She has your eyes."

"I think hers are more beautiful."

"They're both gorgeous. I believe she knows we are here."

"I know she does."

"Do you think she knows we love her?"

"Yes."

Two weeks later, the phototherapy had done its job. Stephanie's liver had had enough time to mature, and hours after Joshua and Scarlet walked into the hospital where they'd left their newborn daughter they walked out with her. Scarlet didn't think her heart could be filled with more love.

As they stepped out onto the steps of the hospital, she paused to gaze up into the sky. She soaked it all in. The sun. The breeze. The touch of her husband's lips to her cheek. The sound of her baby's yawn. All of it brought her peace and joy.

The blessings she'd been given, the blessings she'd lost...all of it was in balance again. The memories of Stephen and Stephen Jr. were still with her, but somehow she knew they would be okay with her moving on with her life in this way.

The wind picked up around them. They hurried to their car.

After bundling their baby in the back and checking twice to make sure the car seat was secure, she slid into the passenger seat beside Josh.

"You ready?" asked Josh.

"I've been ready for a really, really long time. Are you?"

"I've been waiting on you," he smiled.

She leaned over and kissed her husband. "Thank God you came to my rescue."

"You know you rescued me, too."

"You never said that before. How?"

His hand stroked her cheek. "I never thought I would be able to love or trust anyone again, but when you came into my life, I knew there was a chance. And I wanted it."

She caught his hand with hers, and kissed his palm. "Thank you for not giving up on me."

"We're a family."

"Yes..."—she glanced over her shoulder at a sleeping Stephanie—"...we are."

DERAILED

by

Angela Kay Austin

Dedication

This book is for every woman who's ever reached deep into her purse only to find lint and a rusty penny.

Acknowledgements

The inspiration for this book came after watching a news broadcast about troops returning from active zones. The broadcast focused on the difficulty returning vets had with finding jobs and housing. This absolutely amazed me. How can men and women who placed their lives on the line to protect "my" way of life not have a promise that "we" will then provide for them when they are no longer needed on the front lines?

This book is dedicated to the men and women of the military who were placed in harm's way for me. I do not know what I would do if the liberties and opportunities that I have were ever diminished or taken away from me.

Chapter One

"Damn it!" JoAn Fentress sprinted through the traffic of downtown Memphis, TN, not much compared to Nashville, but enough to stop her from reaching her car. "Wait. Wait." The young driver danced to the beat of whatever played through his headphones. He didn't see her flailing her arms, and definitely didn't hear her pleas. He continued to hook her car to the back of his truck.

A gust of wind, powered by the bus barreling down the road beside her, blew her skirt in soft waves around her legs. The faster she ran the more the ankle strap of her shoe slipped. With one misplaced step the shoe twisted, along with her ankle, and the heel snapped. She fell to the cold hard ground beneath her tearing and ripping the papers she carried.

The pain of her ankle pissed her off because she didn't have time for it. Tears filled her eyes, as she stretched her hand toward the tow truck dragging her car away. *Damn! Damn! Damn!* The unwanted crowd of people hovering around assisted her to her feet as they questioned her.

"Are you okay?" asked one short woman watching from nearby with bags of groceries.

She stared at the car wishing for something to happen. Something to stop that truck...to give her a chance to talk to the guy towing it. *No food. No clothes. Nowhere to sleep.* Anger forced the tears she held back to fall. What was she going to do, now?

Derailed

If only the people surrounding her would go away. "Yes, thanks." She sniffed. Annoyed with herself, she picked up her torn papers and, with the help of a young man, tried to stand. "Crap." The sting of the pain traveled through her left leg fast.

"Maybe we should call an ambulance," he said with a question in his voice.

How would she pay for an ambulance or a doctor's examination? "No, I should be fine." Tears fell steadily and heavy, now, she wished she could disappear. If she just had a few minutes to close her eyes and make it all disappear until she could figure out what to do next. "Could you help me to the church on the corner?" she asked. "I just need to sit for a little while, and I'll be okay."

He looked at her, at her tears, at her torn clothes as if he didn't believe her. "Okay."

Day turned to night as she sat on the back pew of the church with no idea what to do next.

"Are you okay, Ma'am?" asked a soft voice from behind her.

JoAn turned to see who'd approached her so quietly. The big bright eyes staring at her were as kind as the voice. "Yes. I'm okay." She searched the night sky through the window beside her. "What time is it?"

The young pre-teen girl checked her watch. "It's almost eight."

"Eight?" The pain in her ankle wasn't as powerful, but the stiffness in her body should've told her it was late. "Is the church closing?"

"No ma'am. We're open all night. Choir practice is about to begin."

"Oh, I should leave." She used the pew in front of her to help her stand. With her torn and soiled papers tucked neatly back into their folder, slowly, she eased from the pew to the aisle. She tried to make her way to the church doors, but the pain of her ankle roared back to life, and she fell to the floor.

The young girl ran to her aid. Together, they were able to get her back to the pew she'd just abandoned. Her movement awoke the rest of her body. The grumbles of her stomach were only slightly covered by the sounds of the members of the congregation pouring into the church.

"That's the choir," said the young girl as she helped her sit. "We eat after rehearsal." The girl's eyes darted towards her stomach before refocusing on her face.

"Thank you, but that's okay." The rumbles of her stomach grew louder, and each one angered her more. The young girl in front of her showered her with that all too familiar pity that irked her as much now, even inside of a church, as it did on the street from adults. With all the strength left inside of her, she wrapped her hands around her torso to muffle the growls, but they fought back and grew louder. "I'll watch for a little while, and then leave."

Members of the choir glanced her way as they entered the church, but for some reason they didn't approach her and ask her to leave. Instead, just like the young girl, they asked her if she needed anything. She'd kill for something to eat, but she told them all no.

At the end of the night, the pastor approached her again. "Are you sure there isn't anything we can do for you?"

"No, thank you." Again, she tried to stand. "I've taken up too much of your time already." The pastor watched her struggle, before he rose to block her path.

"I watched you sleep. You seemed troubled."

"I'm fine. I promise." She glanced at her ankle. "I fell and twisted my ankle. And my car...my car was towed." The energy she'd gathered to stand faded, and she faltered falling unhampered to the hard wood of the pew. A vibration from her impact against the pew traveled down her leg flaring up the pain in her ankle, but she gritted her teeth and swallowed the cry she wanted to yell—for more reasons than her throbbing ankle. The pastor reached for her, but with a nod of her head and a swing of her hand, she dismissed his efforts.

"What can we do to help you?" He placed a hand on top of hers as they rested on her lap.

The warmth of his hand soothed her. His long thin fingers curled round her hands gently squeezing the truth from her lips. "Pastor, I don't know. My car. I don't have...I don't have any place to sleep." He pulled the truth, which she hadn't uttered to many since her discharge from the army, out of her with a few words. Compassion and tenderness poured from his touch and the gentle smile he wore, but no pity—just genuine concern. "I'm sorry to interfere with your choir practice, pastor."

"You haven't interfered." He continued to say good night to members of the church as they filed pass for a hug, a handshake, or a kind word. After the last person was gone, he turned to her. "Well, we can definitely help you with a place to sleep." He stood and reached for her hands. "Let's begin there, and we'll tackle the rest in the morning."

Jo surveyed the small room the pastor had led her to for the night. Tired as she was, she needed a shower. With ease, she removed the only pieces of clothing she owned in the world from her body, and laid them across the bed. In her underwear, she stood in the middle of the room. She had nothing, except the broken shoes that needed to be repaired before her next interview, a pair of ruined stockings, she picked them up and tossed them into a nearby trash can, a skirt, a blouse, and an old blazer.

She went to the bathroom in search of a towel to clean the mud from her shoes. After cleaning them, she searched her purse for her black magic marker. With precision, she filled in the scuff marks, blew a warm breath over the area and repeated the act until all the scrapes were once again covered. Then, she searched the drawers for any type of epoxy glue, but nothing. She'd ask the pastor in the morning.

In the bathroom, she stripped from her underwear, and ran warm sudsy water into the sink. Gently, she washed her belongings in the water. After wringing most of the water from them, she searched the small closet and found a wire clothes hanger. First, she looped one of the bra straps across the hook, and then did the same with her panties. Then she hooked the hanger across the top of the door before returning to the bathroom to shower.

When steam from the shower had fogged the mirror 'til she could no longer see her reflection, she stepped into the shower and let the water beat against her skin. With her face underneath the flow of water, she stood with her hands braced against the wall. It had been awhile since she'd had the privilege of being in a clean shower with plenty of hot water.

She opened her eyes and searched for the soap. Her eyes locked on a single droplet of water. Although she knew it was condensation, she couldn't tear her eyes away. The one droplet slid down the shower until it pebbled with other droplets. They branched out and rolled down the wall. The walls around her were crying. Soon, her own tears followed. *Get it together!*

Jo sprawled out in all directions across... "What...where." Her eyes roamed across the room searching for something familiar. The sound of soft piano music floated through the vents overhead. Her head fell back to the pillow. *The church.* Slowly, her eyes closed.

In protest to the knock on the door, she placed one of the pillows over her head and held it there. Another knock. She sat up, and tossed her feet over the side of the bed. She hated to leave the warmth of the bed, but she guessed the knock on the door signaled her *free* night's stay was over. "One sec. I'll be right there." The underwear wasn't quite dry, so she grabbed the hanger and tossed it into the closet. She pulled on her skirt and blouse. Then, she hobbled around the room searching for her shoes. God, they were trashed. Nothing she could do, but go back to Goodwill and find another pair. She tossed them back to the floor, and answered the door.

An elderly woman, casually dressed, stood just on the other side with a plate of food that could last someone like her for two or three days.

"Good afternoon, young lady. How are you doing today," she said as she slid pass her and walked towards a small table beside a folding chair. She placed the food on the table, and turned toward Jo. "You must've been exhausted." She grinned. "We tried waking you for breakfast, but there was no answer when we knocked." After a quick glance at the table, she continued, "I thought you might be starving."

Jo hated to ignore the woman, and look greedy, but the hollowness inside forced her to practically run to the plate of ham, eggs, and home fries. She plopped into the chair, and took a long deep breath. The salty cheesy warm air filled her lungs, and increased the hunger in her belly. She grabbed the knife and fork, and sliced into the ham. Her stomach growled in anticipation. The salty juices slid down her throat reminding her of what she'd forgotten, *real* food should not be in a can! "Mmm." The pain of losing the cans of tuna in her trunk dulled. She'd think about that tomorrow.

"Thank you."

Jo's hand went to her chest. A few quick taps helped her choke down her delicious bite of ham. "I'm sorry." She glanced at her plate. "I guess I was hungry." She smiled. "Thank you for this. It's delicious." After she quieted the moans of her stomach, she'd pack up some to take with her when she left.

"We cook breakfast and lunch every day for members of the community."

"I've walked past this church a lot. I always see streams of people coming and going." This time she took a bite of food that allowed her to keep talking. "No matter what time of night or day I pass by."

"We're open 24 hours." The woman's infectious smile warmed Jo. "My husband, Pastor Mitchell, never likes to see the doors of the church closed."

"Oh my God, you're the First Lady of this church." Jo choked on the food she shoved into her mouth. "You're bringing me food."

"And I cooked it, too. Don't forget that!" Bell-like laughter rang out from Mrs. Mitchell. When her laughs quieted, she said, "I'm Ms. Velma. Tell me young lady what's your name?"

She'd forgotten. Last night, she was so tired; the pastor had led her to the small room and allowed her to sleep. But, he'd never once asked her if she had a home to go to, or why she was napping on a church pew. "JoAn. JoAn Fentress."

"Fentress. I knew some Fentresses years ago." The woman searched her face as if looking for something. "Did you grow up in Memphis?"

"I lived her for a few years, but I grew up in Nashville."

"Why'd you come back?"

"I don't know." She pushed the plate of food away. "I guess it was the only place I knew to come."

"Do you plan on staying?"

"I don't know."

"Well, if you need a place to stay, you're welcomed to stay here for as long as you need." She headed towards the door. "It's so nice to have young people around."

The room was modest: bare walls, small bed, chair, no TV, but it was bigger than the backseat of her car. But, who lives in a church? "Thank you, but I can't stay here."

"Nonsense. Sure you can. When you finish come downstairs, I'd like you to meet a few people, and..." She eyeballed the broken shoes in the corner. "...maybe we can do something about those shoes."

Barefoot, Jo tiptoed across the cold floors of the church searching for Mrs. Mitchell. Near the top of a narrow staircase laughter floated along the melody of soft piano music. She followed it, and it led her to the person she searched for, as well as, a small group of women.

"Come on over, Jo," said Mrs. Mitchell. She returned her attention to the piano. "Do you sing?"

In the shower. "No."

The women hummed along with the tune Mrs. Mitchell played. Amazed at the beauty of their voices, Jo sat, in a nearby chair, and listened. The words of the song were a testimony. They were thankful. Each word and note saddened her. She couldn't remember the last time she felt thankful.

"Jo, what do you think?" Mrs. Mitchell and the other ladies were staring waiting for a response.

"I'm sorry. I...what do I think about what?"

"Well, we laid some clothes and a few pairs of shoes out for you over there." She pointed. "I wasn't sure about your size, but I thought you might need a few suits or dresses."

Jo ran her hands down the sides of her dress. "No. That's too much. Other people probably need it more than me."

"Well, you take a look, and take whatever you need. The rest we'll put back into our closet for someone else."

If she was going to go to another interview, she definitely needed a pair of shoes. Maybe, she'd just take a look at the shoes. As soon as she had enough money, she could get her car out of the pound. No temp agency would place her, if she walked in looking the way she did. "Okay, I'll take a quick look."

She fingered the collar of a gorgeous black suit. She'd kept a few pieces, but after six months, the clothes she kept had begun to fall apart at the seams. This suit had been worn, but it was better than any of the "make-shift suits" she had in the trunk of her car. "This suit is gorgeous." She looked at Mrs. Mitchell. The older lady's smile brightened. As she lifted the suit from its place on the table, a shoe fell to the ground. *Gorgeous!*

She inspected the shoe as she picked it up from the floor. The buttery rose red leather of the shoe begged her to try it on. Perfect! Not one pinch or tug.

"Jo, that shoe is beautiful on your foot."

She looked at Mrs. Mitchell. "Could I have these along with the suit?"

"Yes. Of course." She turned to the group of waiting women. "We're going to go and finish a little committee business. Take all the time you need to search through everything, and find a few things that work for you."

It didn't matter if she didn't find another thing. The suit and the shoes were plenty. No threads hanging. No holes to stitch. No need for markers to hide the scuff marks. She twirled her foot around in the air. Not markers will be used on these shoes.

The next job she interviewed for was hers!

Chapter Two

"How does a man of your age have absolutely no respect for himself?"

Jeremy briefly glanced away from the television to his mother's disapproving countenance and back before continuing to flip through the television stations until he found what he was searching for. The reporter smiled into the camera as if only for him. And it probably was for him. Moments before her broadcast, she'd been snapping pictures of what was underneath that suit. Pictures he'd love to click through again. He rubbed his fingers across the phone in his pocket. "Respect? I respect myself."

"No. You're coasting your way through life on our money," added his father. "You party all night and weekend. You sleep all day. Until you go to work."

Jeremy had heard enough. The same speech for too many years. "Partying all night." They still didn't understand. "It's my job to 'party.' I'm an entertainment reporter."

"You can report the news without becoming it." His father threw a copy of the paper on the table. Right there was a picture of his smiling face with his arms draped around two women. Shit, he didn't even really remember the women's names. They were at the function he'd attended a few days earlier to raise money for something...homeless or was it for some children's cause?

"Okay. Okay. I get it. I'll change." That's all they ever wanted to hear him say.

Derailed

"You're not a college kid any more. It's time for you to grow up, Jeremy," said his mother.

This was new. "What are you talking about?"

"It's time for you to grow up, son." His father handed him some papers. "We've set up a small...very small bank account for you." The hand on his shoulder felt familiar, but something was different. "With your job at the television station and the money in this account, you can do it."

"Do what?" He ripped the envelop open. Anger boiled inside of him as he read the pages. "You want me to live off this."

"Son, your sister is getting married." His father looked at his mother. "We're getting older."

"Dad. It's not like I'm picking up hookers. Just a little harmless fun."

His mother fell to the couch in tears as she spoke. "We're tired, baby. The drinking. The women."

"Mom..." His head swiveled back and forth between his parents. "Dad come on."

His dad turned his attention to his mother. They were the only two people he knew who were still on their first marriage. As a kid, he remembered them always showing their affection: holding hands, kissing, and acting like teenagers in love. They still did those things.

As his father wrapped his arms around his mother, he said, "Son, we love you. But, it's time you grew up."

It'd been weeks since Jeremy had had any real conversations with his parents. They were focused on his sister's wedding, and they hadn't changed their tune about *his* money or *his* job. They had no idea what it took to do his job. They, his father mainly, thought it was another way for him to keep the party going from college. Women. Drinks. Parties. But, it wasn't. Photojournalism ad always been his thing, changing the world through his pictures, but no one took the wealthy pretty boy seriously. So, he gave them what they wanted.

He stood on the stage staring into the crowd. How many of these events did he emcee every year? They were all beginning to blur together. Not that they weren't worthy causes, but with all the money he helped these groups raise every year, how many homeless people were left in Memphis?

He unsealed the envelope and hunched down to read the name of the next honoree (they never had a mic long enough for him to stand straight). He watched the old couple slowly navigate the stairs. They'd been honored many times by various organizations across Memphis. Their little church was historic. It'd sat in downtown Memphis for two generations serving anybody in need. If he remembered correctly, the current pastor's wife's father began the church in his backyard in one of the rougher parts of town, but finally raised enough money to open the church, and it's doors have been open ever since.

As the pastor neared to take the envelope and the award, he realized the older gentlemen's age had given a slight curve to his posture, without it, he would've challenged Jeremy's own 6'2". His wife, however, was petite and adorable. With a head full of snowy grey hair, her chocolate skin glistened underneath the lights bringing more attention to his fading tan. He stepped to the side to allow them to speak. "We thank you all for this honor..." Jeremy scanned the audience for possible companions for the evening. Blondes. Brunettes. Red heads. They smiled, and he smiled back, but not with any interest. Habit.

Not that they weren't fun. But, over the years the *high* he got from the women he shared his bed with wore off faster and faster. It didn't matter if it were one or two there was still something he could only describe as boredom that came crashing down on him the instant he came. Usually, he'd throw back another drink, try it again, or fuck it and leave.

The pastor and his wife finished their remarks, and he robotically moved back to his place behind the podium.

Derailed

At the end of the night, Jeremy stood with Tim, his camera guy, recapping the night.

"Not sure about this night, Tim"

"It was good," he hesitated, "but we could definitely use one more shot that wraps it up."

"Exactly. Something that puts a face on this that people can relate to. Not shots of wealthy people eating bad food." He knew that by the time Tim finished editing it, it'd make anyone dig into their pockets and give, but one more shot would be good for him and the cause.

Luck was watching over him. The pastor and his wife came strolling by. "Excuse me." The pastor and his wife waited. "Could I get a comment from you both for the late night news?"

The pastor's wife smoothed down her hair and tugged at her dress with a big smile. "We'd love to."

"Velma, do we have time?"

"Sure. Our ride won't be here for awhile."

She looped her hand through her husband's arm, and asked "What do you need us to do?"

"Nothing. This will be easy. I'll just ask you a few questions, and that's it." He cued his camera man. "With me this evening Pastor Mitchell and his wife of Mt. Zion Baptist Church. Pastor, your wife, and your church have been honored several times for your work in the community. Can you tell us more about it?"

"My father-in-law was a great man. He grew up in Memphis when things were much more difficult than they are today. And he had a vision." As he spoke his wife's grip on his arm tightened, and her smile broadened. She loved her husband, and respected him and her father. They reminded Jeremy of his own parents. Finding that kind of love was rare and damn near impossible. "We'd love to have you come down and see what we do," finished the pastor.

He didn't even know what the old man had asked him to come and see. "I'd love to. Just tell me when and where."

"We're holding a big Valentine's Day dinner for the neighborhood. It's going to be great!" said Mrs. Mitchell.

"I'll be there."

Jeremy and his camera man packed everything into the truck. There wasn't much. Without a lot of thought, he twisted the mic chords into a huge figure eight and banded them with their own chords as he ran a play by play of the night ahead through his mind. Shit. He adjusted himself to shift the weight of the bulge growing in the front of his pants.

Blood rushed to all the right places prepping him as he shut the doors of the truck. But, a dull nagging pulled at him. He knew as soon as that craving was satisfied the emptiness would return again. As he waited on his camera man to finish, he saw the old couple trot down the front stairs of the banquet hall, where they'd been waiting since he interviewed them. A blue mini-van slid up to the curb in front of them, and the drivers' side door opened.

The woman who emerged from within didn't wear a coat, just a snuggly fitted jacket. The long skirt she wore hugged her hips and bottom, nicely. Each move of her body spoke to his. Long legs strolled up to the curb. *Damn!* Petite red shoes stepped up on the sidewalk. The pastor and his wife hugged her, as if they hadn't seen her in years. Jeremy couldn't see her face, but he could tell from their expressions that she was smiling, too. They hugged and kissed her until she forced them into the van. The longer she took to turn and show her face, the more he wanted to see it. *Her.*

"Jeremy, are you ready?"

The voice came from behind him. He spun to acknowledge her. "Almost." He turned his attention back to the van too late. The drivers' door closed, and the van pulled away. *Damn!* Tim and his *lady in waiting* watched him as he watched the van drive off. He tried to shake off the curiosity that didn't want him to turn away. "Tim, you got it from here?" he asked.

"Got it, man." The man was a whiz with a camera, any kind, but never really said much. They'd worked together since Jeremy's first day at the station. He'd saved Jeremy's ass in a lot of ways, a lot of times. Tim was the only person he really cared to work with on a shoot.

He looked at his *lady in waiting*. A slow lick of her lips was her response. Wrapping his arm around her waist, he focused on her, but he still couldn't erase the thoughts of the other woman from his mind. The way her body moved excited him in a way he hadn't been for a long time. His date cozied up closer as they walked.

She looked up into his eyes. "Do you think you can stay over, tonight?"

A simple question. It should be an easy thing, but it wasn't. "I have some early edits." If he stayed, he knew how that would go. She'd wake up early, cook breakfast, talk about what kind of a future they could have together. Make plans for *their* future. He didn't have any answers about the future, his, hers, or theirs.

"It's been a long time since we've seen each other. It would be nice to wake up with you beside me." She stopped walking, and waited.

He let his fingers caress the side of her face as he spoke. "I'm sorry. You know my sister's getting married, and with the job I haven't had a lot of free time." Her stare softened. "Maybe after this wedding is over, I'll have more time." He pulled her head back and kissed her. Her moans as he deepened his kiss told him she accepted his answer.

Satisfied, she smiled. They walked to the car without her bothering him with questions.

Chapter Three

Too much scotch! At the protest of his latest conquest, he tucked in his shirt, and snapped up his pants.

"Why do you have to leave so early?" she asked.

He stuffed his feet into his loafers, and crammed his socks into his pocket as he grabbed his jacket. "I told you..." He patted his pockets for his wallet and keys. "Where are my keys?" She pointed at a dresser on the other side of the room. "My producer is really riding my ass about this one. I should've been in the studio an hour ago." He headed towards the door.

Sitting up in bed, she asked, "When will I see you again?" The sheet she covered herself with fell to her waist exposing her breasts.

If it hadn't been for the scotch, he would've left last night. As he stood there sober staring at her: sex hair, flashing him her breasts, he wanted to run. "I'll call you," he barked over his shoulder. "I promise."

Freshly showered and suited, a few hours later, Jeremy strolled through the halls of WLRP. He stopped at Susie's desk. "Hey beautiful." He smiled. "Could you do something for me?" he asked.

She smiled back. "Yellow, or white...roses, or daisies?" Secretaries that would help you hide a body were hard to find. That was his team: Susie and Tim.

Derailed

"You decide." He turned to walk away. "Ginger." A soft gasp at that name halted his steps, briefly. But, then he heard her make a few clicks on her keyboard before she spoke again. "Yes, I'd like to send your biggest bouquet of daisies to Ginger at..." her voice trailed off as he walked further down the hall.

Before he could find Tim, he needed to see what was waiting for him on his desk, and pop his head into his producer's office. Lately, the man reminded him of his parents. Nothing he did was good enough.

The voice sighing into his voicemail was the same one he'd just left half-naked in bed. The press of one button, and he deleted her request to come back for dinner.

"Jeremy."

At the sound of his name, he placed the phone back in its cradle, and looked up at Neal, his producer. "I was on my way to see you."

The man's expression never seemed to change, lately. He glanced around the room without speaking.

He continued, "We're working on the footage from last night. It'll be good for tonight's broadcast."

"Good. But, that's not why I'm here." Neal closed the door behind him, and leaned against it. "What are you doing, Jeremy?"

Shit. "What do you mean?"

"When I hired you for this...this job...I knew it wasn't what you really wanted, but my relationship with your parents and with you made me take a chance." He walked to a nearby chair and sat. "You never liked it, but you respected it. Now, I don't think you even respect it."

"Neal, I respect you and this job. I show up every day. I never turn down an assignment."

Neal threw up his hands in protest. "That's not what I'm talking about." He stopped. "I don't care what assignment I give you, you find a way to turn it into a party."

"I have a little fun once in a while, but it's on my time, not yours."

"Damn it, Jeremy." Neal emphasized his disapproval by slamming his right fist into the palm of his left hand. "Did you really think screwing the daughter of the fucking lead anchor would be a good idea?"

"We dated in high school," he slung out one arm, and knocked a lamp off his desk. He left it where it fell. "I didn't make her any promises. I've been in that bed a few times since high school."

Neal stood. "This was the last." With his hand on the doorknob, he said, "Out of respect for your parents, I put my neck on the line for you. Don't make me regret it. I need to see something different from you, or this time will be the last time."

Jeremy dragged himself into editing with Tim. Neal's words were still fresh in his mind. The damn man didn't have to admit that the job was given to him because of his parents. He didn't need his help or his parents'. His degrees didn't come with a price tag. Scholarships for both grad and undergrad, and he'd worked his ass off for them, too.

"Hey, man," said Tim as he walked into the editing suite.

"How are we looking? Enough worthwhile?" He dropped into a chair to watch Tim work his magic.

"We're looking good." He hit a few buttons, and the edited version of the footage from the night before began to play.

Over the next hours, they cleaned up a few spots throughout the piece. The playback on the last few minutes of the segment gave him an idea.

Chapter Four

Crap. Crap. Crap. Jo dashed out of the building to the van the church gave her. She was late. She knew Pastor would be waiting at the door with his hands crossed as soon as she arrived.

She raced through the streets, carefully. No sense in hurting herself or anyone else, but there was nothing she could do. She had a huge learning curve with the new job. The church had a lot of friends. Most of them actually worked with the church because they loved what the church did for the community. And she did, too.

They did what you'd expect: gave out food, clothes, and things like that. But, they also helped with job placement, and had a clinic for low income families in the community. Of course, they wouldn't take no for an answer when she refused their offer of a job. So, she took a job as manager of their outreach programs, which combined efforts of the church and clinic.

If you looked at it the way she did, she was late because she loved them, and she didn't want to let them down. But, that would never work with the pastor.

She pulled the van up to the church lot and parked. The motion light at the side door announced her arrival, and the pastor met her at the top of the steps. Like a 16-year old breaking curfew, after a quick peck on the cheek, she slinked pass him.

"Young lady, you're late." He closed the door behind them.

"Pastor, do you know how many appointments I had today?"

"Yes. That's why we needed you."

Again, she doubted her ability. She had no degrees. And if it hadn't been for her military deployments, she'd probably have never left Tennessee, let alone the country. God, she was thankful. "Your wife was supposed to work with me today, but you stole her from me."

"Who else did you think would organize this dinner tonight?"

"Okay. Okay, you win." She threw up both hands in a sign of resignation. "Where do you need me?"

He smiled. "Emcee. Of course."

"Wait? What?"

"Well, this event is a fundraiser for the clinic and the outreach programs. Who would be better to emcee, than you?" He placed a hand on each shoulder and squeezed.

"I thought I'd be..." She humped her shoulders in the air. "Rubbing elbows with the guests."

He laughed. "That's my job."

With her dress and shoes in hand, she walked to her old familiar room to prepare for the evening.

Jeremy helped Tim place one camera in the back of the fellowship hall. Tim had another with him and, tonight, he had one of his favorite still shot cameras, too. He caressed the leather bag containing one of the first cameras his sister had bought him. She'd always supported his love of photography. She'd been one of his first models. Along with their pets, weather, and anything that couldn't run. But, he loved taking pictures of people. Telling stories with his photographs burned hot in him until he quieted—ignored—that voice when he took the job at the station. He didn't expect much from the evening, outside of the ordinary; but, he would be prepared, and somewhere deep inside of him a spark that he barely recognized began to smolder.

While Tim finished the set-up in the back, he walked around testing the light in the room. After a brief conversation with the pastor and his wife, he waited off-stage for the evening to begin. Focused on Pastor Mitchell, he waited for him to approach the stage. Only after the woman had already stepped behind the podium did her voice alert him that he'd missed something.

No shot. Shadowed off-stage, he snapped a few pics of the audience. The expression on the face of the pastor and his wife, priceless. They stared at the speaker with the pride of parents. After a short opening, she turned, and Jeremy's camera slipped from his hands. The neck strap saved it from crashing to the floor. The horrible low lighting of the church couldn't dampen her beauty.

The crappy lights dimmed further, but still he noticed. Long black hair framing her face bobbed softly with each step she took. For a quick moment, too quick, their eyes met, but she tore her eyes from his when she turned towards the audience. He watched as she...what...those shoes...it's *her*!

He nearly ran down the stairs after her, but why? He'd seen a lot of beautiful women. Most of them ended up in his bed. But, this one hadn't, yet. However, on many many nights, she'd been in his head wearing nothing but those red shoes.

Instead of disturbing the audience's view of the video that began when she left the podium, he walked through a side door, and reentered the hall from the rear. An empty seat beside the pastor and his wife was now filled with his mystery woman. He focused his camera's eye on her. Through his lens she was more beautiful. Creamy brown skin, full lips, bright eyes. His trigger finger snapped shot after shot.

At the conclusion of the video, the pastor, his wife, and *his* mystery woman took their places center stage. They spoke, but he didn't know what was said. Shot after shot, he captured the entire moment on film.

When they left the stage, he met them. "Pastor, this was a great evening."

"Well…" The pastor nodded at Jeremy's mystery woman. "…it's not over, yet." The woman stepped a little closer to them. "This is Jo. She made all of this happen."

Jo. Jeremy watched as Jo's smile broadened and her complexion tinted softly darker at the pastor's words.

"Pastor, it wasn't just me." Jo hugged the pastor's wife. "Ms. Velma did a lot. We're a team."

Jeremy placed his camera to his eye. "Would you mind if I take a few shots?"

"I'd love it," answered the pastor. He placed his arms around both women.

After he took a few pictures of them, he asked, "So, what's next."

"Dinner," Jo responded. "The choir will sing. It's an extravaganza!" She laughed.

Glancing over his shoulder, he said, "Give me a minute." He walked to where Tim was busy packing up everything to move it to the next position. "I think I can handle it from here."

"You sure?" This had to be the first time he'd actually felt like he'd stumped the man of little words.

He patted the other camera hanging on his shoulder. "Yeah, got it covered."

"Then, I'm out of here." He went back to breaking down the camera. "My wife will love me coming home early."

"Alright." He turned to walk back to the waiting group. "I'll catch you in the morning. I want this one to have more of a documentary feel, not slick."

After a brief pause, Tim responded, "Okay."

He followed the trio into another room.

"Jeremy, we normally use this room for overflow crowds on Sundays or during the holidays when we have huge crowds for our meal program," said Ms. Velma.

The room was decorated with images of happy people smiling, eating, in hospital beds. As they walked, he trailed them until they stopped in front of a small stage.

"The Praise Steppers will perform here after the choir, while we eat," said Jo.

They sat at the only empty table in the room. No reserved signs marked the table, but everyone left it untouched. He hesitated, but then at the nod of the pastor, he sat. Servers placed food at all the tables. The smells of catfish, greens, and yams circulated through the room. But, the dish they sat in front of him wasn't what he expected. With his fork, he checked the layers: greens on the bottom, catfish nestled on top them, and then thin slices of cinnamon kissed yams. He could barely wait to dig in.

The pastor stood, and someone handed him a microphone. A simple blessing of the food before they ate. As a kid, his family barely ever ate together. His parents were loving, but his father worked too much, and his mother filled her time with every volunteer organization and school organization she found worthy.

"I hope you like the food," Jo whispered to him. Her soft floral scented perfume wrapped around him, pulling him in closer. "The caterer is a member of our church, and for awhile used many of the services we offer to the community."

He grabbed his camera, and snapped. She blinked. "Sorry, but that was a great shot." He placed the camera at his feet, and focused on the people at his table. "How do you know the pastor and his wife?"

For a moment, she stared at the pastor and his wife, and then she answered, "They saved me."

Chapter Five

Picture after picture, she smiled from the screen at him. Jeremy couldn't help but smile back at her. Although she smiled, her eyes had been touched by pain. They were filled with wisdom. The pictures of Jo with the pastor and his wife could only be described as love. Pure love. He didn't think they had any children. At least, none he'd ever seen or heard of.

Neal, his producer, had agreed to give him a little more time than normal to work on this piece. He'd promised to give him something different. The fundraiser was not *different*. He needed more. Didn't someone mention a clinic? What about the pictures of the hospital beds on the wall? Maybe, there was more to the little 24-hour church on the corner. He picked up his bag, and headed out of the apartment.

At the steps of the church, Jeremy paused as he adjusted his jacket and raked a shaky hand through his hair, slightly longer now. He always let it grow a little longer in the winter. The church door opened before he reached it. An older man, loaded down with packages, walked carefully down the stairs.

"Do you need help?" asked Jeremy.

"I've got it." He smiled. "Thank you."

"Jeremy..."

He looked up at the sound of his name. Mrs. Mitchell. "Hello." He raised his camera. "Would this be an okay time to take a few more shots?"

"We don't have anything going on today, except our Clothes Closet, and we'll be serving dinner a little later." She closed the door behind him. "But, you're welcome to take pictures as long as people are okay with being in them."

"Didn't someone mention a clinic to me," he asked. He hated that he couldn't remember who'd actually told him of the program. "I'd love to visit it if possible. I have another camera in the car. Maybe, I could get a few shots and some footage."

"Oh, I think the pastor would love that!" She took him by the hand, and dragged him along behind her. "Let's find him."

"I thought..."

"Wait, we'll discuss it with my husband and Jo."

"Jo." The little woman stopped tugging him like a rag doll, and turned to stare.

"Jo handles the outreach programs for us. She's focused a lot on the clinic and veteran's needs since she joined us."

"Veterans?"

"She's ex-military. Army. She served in Afghanistan."

Afghanistan. "How did she begin working with you here at the church?"

She turned away, and tightened her grip on his hand. "I'll let her tell you how we became so blessed. Let's find my husband, and then we'll go meet Jo."

The quartet strolled through the halls of the clinic. "How does the clinic work?" Jeremy asked.

"We partnered with the health department's health loop program," Jo responded. "It allows us to provide convenient quality healthcare services," she concluded.

"But, the addition of programs for women veterans was all Jo." The pastor beamed. "The U.S. Veterans Initiative has a lot on its plate."

"You only help women veterans?" he asked.

"We won't turn away anyone that needs help," Jo answered, "But, women veterans have fewer resources. There were over 200,000 women serving in Iraq and Afghanistan. On average 20 percent of female veterans have military sexual trauma that result in mental illness, alcoholism, depression, or physical illness."

"I had no idea," Jeremy said.

"Most people don't." She wrapped an arm around the pastor. "And like Pastor said, the U.S. Veterans Initiative can't do it all. They only have about 11 sites all in major cities around the country."

"To help our community, we have developed programs for unemployment, hunger, homelessness, and counseling for physical and mental traumas," added Mrs. Mitchell.

"The fundraiser helps with those initiatives?" he asked.

"Yes. The partnership with the health department helps with some of the costs, but the fundraisers and partnerships with businesses within the community are what will help us keep all of the services going," added Jo.

"Jo," the pastor interrupted, "we're going to head back to the church. We need to make sure things are set for this evening's meals program." They each hugged her and then turned to him. "Come on by if you'd like to take a few pictures of the program tonight or any night."

"Make plans with Jo, she knows our schedule and every program inside and out," said Mrs. Mitchell.

"Thank you, I will." Jeremy turned to Jo. "Do you mind if I trail around behind you for the rest of the day? I'd like to get a few more pictures."

"Okay, but I'm starved." She patted her flat stomach. "How about we get something to eat?"

Jeremy thought he'd eaten in every restaurant in Memphis, but this little place nestled right off Beale Street surprised him. A two man band sang with the influence of Sinatra. Not the typical Memphis set, but jazzy and heartfelt.

Over a plateful of ribs, he quizzed her. "Before you said the pastor and his wife saved you." He sipped from his sweet tea. "It seems like it was mutual."

She smiled. "Maybe a little."

"How'd they save you?"

"Well, I guess..." She frowned. The crinkles in her forehead emphasized her question. "Wait, is all of this going into your project?"

He wasn't thinking about the project at the moment. The question was for him. Something inside of him hungered to know her. He splayed his hands for her to see. "No camera, no pad for notes. Just a conversation."

"I served in Afghanistan." She rubbed a hand down her right leg. "I was wounded. After that, I was placed on medical discharge."

"I thought women didn't serve combat posts," he paused, and scanned her body, closely. For the first time, he searched her for signs of injury, instead of curiosity. "How close were you to combat?" Questions raced through his mind. "How severely were you wounded?"

"Yeah, you're right. Even though the rules have flexed a bit to allow women to serve closer to the front lines, policy still bans us from being assigned to units below the brigade level. Army and Marines are stricter on women than Air Force and Navy, mainly because of the infantry positions." Again, she rubbed her thigh. "That policy barred women from serving in infantry or special operations where the heavy action and immediate danger can be found. But, we're still close enough to it to be wounded and discharged," she answered.

Normally, clear and bright, her eyes fogged. The strength he'd admired in her throughout the day vanished, and the woman sitting across from him was exposed. Still strong, but vulnerable. Her carefully crafted façade cracked. And he saw a glimpse of what he could only describe as pain. Not from the thigh she kept rubbing, but from something deeper.

"Is that what brought you to the church?"

"No." She laughed, somberly. The crack he'd glimpsed for a moment had sealed. "I hobbled into the church one day after my car was towed away. It was the only place I could think of to go."

"What...you didn't have a home?"

She stopped eating, and stared at him. "Does that surprise you?" Her expression challenged him.

He didn't want to offend her. Concern for her and her safety shaped his questions and thoughts. "Yes. You were...are a veteran."

Beautiful brown eyes searched his face for something. Then she spoke, "Did you know that minority veterans are the largest percentage of homeless veterans?"

"How is that possible?"

"A lot of minorities enter into the military to get away. Less education. Bad neighborhoods. Few or bleak opportunities." She sat her fork down, and rested back in her chair. "That's why so many find themselves in the same position I was in. When I was discharged, I lost half of my salary. That didn't allow me to take care of myself."

"But, what about the initiative?"

"It helps, but it really can't do everything. The current administration wants to erase veteran homelessness over the next three years. That's great, but how?"

"Programs and money." His lack of knowledge on the subject embarrassed him.

"Okay, but women veterans have issues slightly different from men. And the programs that exist try to handle all of our issues the same way. You can't do that." She pointed at herself. "We need programs that help us."

He stared at his sweet tea wishing for something stronger. "Why didn't you go to your family for help?"

"That's not always an option for everyone," she paused. "It wasn't for me."

Why wasn't her family an option? More than before the armor she wore closed around her. When it came to reading women, he never had a problem. This time...this woman was different. He couldn't read a thing.

"But..."

"Enough about me, let's get back to the program." She grabbed her fork, and dived back into her salad.

"Do you have many business partners?"

"The church has been around a long time. We've developed our own chamber of commerce. There are currently 50 local businesses that support us."

"Between health loop and the church's chamber of commerce are all your programs financially healthy?"

"Most of them, but the addition of women's veterans programs is causing a bit of a strain. We may have to restructure a few of the programs." That frown he was growing to hate returned to her brow. "We'd wanted to expand and add a shelter for women vets and their families this year, but it may not be possible until we find a few more partners."

"What about loans? Where would the shelter be located?"

"I'm not sure. With this economy there are a lot of properties available, but we haven't been able to qualify for a loan. We may need to raise the money to buy the property outright. But, then we wouldn't have the ability to do the necessary repairs."

The most he'd done was emcee the events for groups that sent requests to the station. If he were honest, he picked the event based on how many single women might attend. This woman had lived through who knows what, and now, she'd dedicated herself to giving something back. No bitterness or anger colored her words or actions. He'd be mad as hell if he'd gone through what she had. That dull ache deep inside grew stronger. He didn't know what to do to make it go away. "It's a worthy program."

"Yes, but I don't want any of the church's other programs to suffer for this one," a soft sadness filled her words. "The meals and clinic programs are just as necessary. The clinic's programs help us with a lot of our women's vets' services providing therapists and clinicians."

The ache inside of him beat a fist against his chest. "Maybe, I can help you find partners."

"How?" Her eyes latched onto his and something inside of him decided he would do anything to see *that* again.

"I've worked with every person of power in this city. The piece I've been working on was for the news, but what if we do something more?"

95

"Like what?" she asked. Her face lit up with anticipation at his next words.

"We could extend the idea into a documentary and maybe a book. The money could go towards your fundraising efforts."

The smile that spread across her face fed that ache inside of him. *What was that?* It scared him a little, jolted him. He didn't think he would be able to face the possibility of having *that* feeling taken away from him. He liked it and wanted to feel *that*, whatever it was, again.

Chapter Six

Jo pulled out her hand mirror to reapply her lipstick before Jeremy's arrival. He'd promised to meet them at their *wish* site to get more footage for the documentary. She managed to find five women that agreed to allow him to interview them on-camera. They didn't want their full names used, but they were all excited to discuss the issues concerning women veterans. They were all willing to do whatever it took to help the church get the women's shelter completed.

She hopped out of the car, and joined the women who sat bundled in coats and scarves at a long wooden bench. They smiled and greeted her. Rounding the table, she hugged and kissed each one.

Jeremy darted across the yard in her direction. She waited for him to get closer before she spoke. "Did you have a hard time finding this place?"

"No, I was stuck in the studio wrapping up some edits." He smiled. "I think it's really coming together."

"Do you really?" She searched the women's faces. "You're not just saying that to make us feel good, and get our hopes up are you?"

"No." He took a few steps closer. The warmth of her nearness flowed into him. "I wouldn't want to disappoint any of you."

She'd hoped the shelter wasn't turning out to be a big mistake. The church could use it. The women around the table could use it. And, if she were being totally honest, she could use it, too. "Well, in that case take a seat." She sat and motioned towards a seat beside her. "Ask away."

"First," he opened his satchel, and pulled out cameras of different sizes. "I'm going to set up one camera, and take a few still shots." He searched the women's expressions. "Is that okay with everyone?"

"I told them you might want pictures. We're all okay, but don't forget...no last names."

"No problem." He walked around tapping the ground with his foot searching for a level spot to set-up. He decided on one spot, and placed his tripod. After setting the camera, he turned to the women. "Ladies, the camera is rolling. I'll ask questions off camera, and if something feels good, I'll take pictures, too."

He pointed the camera that he held at Carmen. "Can you tell me why you think this shelter would be important to you, or why it's necessary?"

After a pause and a quick scan of the table, she responded softly, "When I enlisted it was because I couldn't afford to go to college." Her hands twisted around themselves on top of the table. "It was a way for me to get out of my parents house and take care of myself. But after a few tours, I couldn't take it anymore. The men that worked with me didn't respect me." Her eyes fell to the table. "Reporting them got me nothing. Drinking helped me escape from all of it. I haven't been able to hold a job."

Veronica jumped in. "When we come back, we all have problems of all kinds, but not for the same reasons as men. But, when they try to help us...they help us like they would a man."

"We may have some of the same symptoms, but the reasons why are different," added Jessica. "I have a daughter, but without being able to get a better paying job, we're renting a room." Tears fell. "What am I supposed to tell her 'serve your country, and this is what you get?'"

Cindy added, "I was proud of my service, but after I left active duty, I couldn't find a job that allowed me to use my skills from the military. They all loved my military clearance, but none of them thought I was qualified to do anything."

Laurie's bright red face showed her anger. "I couldn't believe after my husband died that it would be so hard to try to survive on only my income. I was always so careful with money."

After the women's voices died down, Jeremy continued, "But, why this shelter? Don't programs like this already exist?"

Jo spoke, "Sure programs exist, but not enough. There are a lot of women waiting."

"Jo turned down housing for one of our friends who had a baby only a few months old," added Carmen.

All the women nodded in Jo's direction, and gently smiled at Carmen's words.

"The problem with the programs that exist is that they can't help all the women who need it, and they're focused on the larger cities." Jo continued, "Right here in our own hometown, there aren't resources dedicated specifically to women. The pastor and the church realized this when they offered me a place to live and a job." She stared into the camera that rested against his face. "They saved me. I don't know what I would've done if the church hadn't been open that day."

Derailed

The drive home took longer than normal. Jeremy drove the car into the driveway, and dragged his gear and himself to the front door. He pulled his key from his pocket, and stuck it in the lock. The door was stuck. He sat his gear on the ground beside him, and jiggled the key around. He couldn't remember his door ever jamming before tonight.

Light from the inside of the house hit him in the eyes, and he blinked. His father? What was he...

"Jeremy, what are you doing?"

"What?" Damn. He'd driven home to his parents' house instead to his own. "Sorry."

"Are you drunk?"

"No." He picked up his gear and headed to his car.

"Jeremy." He heard his mother's soft voice. "Stay for awhile. We haven't seen you in such a long time." He turned to her. Brunette hair that never faded framed her face. Soft wrinkles had begun to slightly touch her forehead and deepen around her mouth. Now, they were enhanced from worry for him, but he was certain they originally came from laughter. There was hardly a time he could remember from his childhood that she wasn't laughing. Even when he knew she missed his father the most. If he had a problem with taking life too seriously, he was sure it stemmed from some twisted view of watching how much his mom enjoyed everything: food, travel, music. He wanted to enjoy life, too.

"Sorry Mom, I'm working on a project." Her light sigh broke his heart, and changed his mind. "I have to look at some footage. I guess I could do it here."

"Wonderful." She pushed her husband to the side, and as Jeremy approached the door, she wrapped her arms around him. After she placed a soft warm peck on his cheek, she said "I've missed you, hon. Tell us all about your project."

"This one is tougher than I thought it would be, but I'm proud of it."

"What is it about this time?" asked his father. "College sorority girls gone wild?"

"No, it's about homeless women veterans." His father's expression changed. Jeremy didn't know how to describe it, but, maybe, it was curiosity. He kept talking. "Y'all know that church downtown that's open 24 hours?" He took their silence as a yes. "I've been working with Jo, a woman from the church, on putting together a short documentary that will chronicle their attempts at setting up a shelter."

"Son, that's a wonderful idea." His mother beamed as she clapped her hands together.

"I thought so, too, but I didn't know until tonight that Jo was a homeless vet, too. She was injured during the war, and her medical disability didn't allow her to take care of herself."

"Son, that's...I don't know...that's..." his mother couldn't finish.

His father didn't speak, just sat listening.

"She had an opportunity to receive housing, but gave it up for another woman who had a child. For months, she lived out of her car until it was towed, and the church was the only place she could think of to go."

"It sounds like she owes them a lot," his father finally commented.

"I think she thinks so, too, but she does it because she believes in it." He unpacked his camera. "Would y'all like to see the interview?"

Both his parents responded, "Yes."

When the video finished, his mother asked, "How is this possible?"

"I don't know."

"They served the country, and now they can't feed their children, find jobs, or find a place to live. This is unbelievable. There must be more to this."

"I don't know, mom." He repacked his stuff. "I've been interviewing members of the church and community, there's tons of footage you haven't seen. This is true."

"Then, we have to help you," his father announced.

Jeremy, his mother, and his father strolled with Jo, the pastor and his wife through the empty sanctuary.

"I never knew this church had such beautiful markings," said his mother. "All these years, and I've never been inside."

"When my father finally had enough money to buy it, he said he wanted people to feel they were surrounded by love. But, he didn't want it to be overdone," Mrs. Mitchell reminisced as her eyes bounced off the various carvings in the room. Unspoken memories of her father and her childhood seemed to flutter through her mind. "I guess that's why most of the work was done by him and some of the members of the church."

"What? Your father did this beautiful wood work?" Jeremy's mom slid her fingers across a nearby piece of sculpture."

"Not all of it, but a lot." She beamed with pride as she continued to scan the walls and ceilings of the church. "His father told him a man should always know how to work with his hands. It was his trade."

The pastor grabbed her in a bear hug and squeezed. "I think she thought she'd found a man like her father when she met me." He kissed her on her cheek.

"Why?" asked Jeremy's mother.

"When we met, I worked in construction." He glanced at his now thin curved fingers. "But, after meeting her father, and witnessing his good work, I knew." He stretched his arms out wide, and looked up. "This is where I was supposed to be, and this is what I was supposed to do with my life."

"I thought I was rebelling, but look at me," Ms. Velma's smile stretched from ear to ear.

And so did Jo's. She took as much pride as they did in the church, and its history.

"Jo, I threw around a few ideas with Jeremy about how we could get involved with your fundraising efforts," began his mother. "He wanted us to discuss them with you."

"We love that you are willing to help, Mrs. Hooks," Jo responded.

"Oh please, call me Floydette and..." She pointed at his dad. "Call him Milton."

Jo's soft smile and head nod were her only response.

"Jo, mom and dad know everybody in Memphis. They would be able to hold a huge fundraiser for the church."

"I think it's a wonderful idea, but where would we hold the event?" Jo asked.

"Why can't we have it in the fellowship hall?" asked Mrs. Velma.

"If we're going to have an event with dinner and drinks, similar to the program you attended where we met Jeremy, we should have it off-site," Jo answered.

His mom turned to the pastor and his wife. "I think Jo's right. We want this one to be more party-like." She smiled. "People will give a lot more money if they're at a party."

His father jumped in. "We won't do anything that will embarrass the church, but Jeremy will finish the documentary, and we could show and sell it at the event.

Along with the cost of entry benefiting the shelter and the church."

"Pastor, what do you think?" Jo asked.

"If we monitor the liquor and use our meals program and members of our jobs program for staff needs," he answered. "I think it'll work."

"I think that's a lovely idea," his mother said. "The people donating will see some of the people their money will help."

"Pastor, do you think they will want to work the fundraiser?" asked Jo.

"I think if people are going to donate, they should know who they're donating to," he answered. "And more of the donations will come back to the church, not pay bills."

His mother clapped her hands together. "Wonderful. Jo, can you introduce me to a few people that I'll need to know to work out some of the details?" She looped her arm around Jo's and dragged her away from the small crowd.

Jeremy's father smiled at the disappearing image of his mother. "Your mother loves planning any event."

"Well, then she'll love our Jo," added Ms. Velma. "Just as much as we do." She elbowed Jeremy in the stomach.

His father stared at the exchange without a sound.

Chapter Seven

Jo handed Jeremy a bowl of popcorn.

"Well, if we're going to watch a movie, I figured we had to do it right." She smiled the most beautiful smile a woman had ever given him the pleasure of witnessing.

He took the bowl. "Thank you."

"So, this film doesn't show us as a bunch of crazy religious zealots, does it?"

The popcorn he'd just thrown in his mouth choked him. When he could speak, he said, "No. I think the world of you, the pastor and his wife...this church."

"Do you?" She waited for a response.

"The work this church does isn't only necessary, but important." He leaned back into his chair. "I didn't realize so many people you walk by every day needed something in their lives, and had no resource to turn to." He leaned a little closer to her. "I thought of homeless people like characters in a movie. Living on the street in cardboard boxes, addicts...but, in my mind, it was always their own fault. I never took the time to understand why. This has opened my eyes."

"I'm glad." She searched his eyes. "You're a good person, Jeremy. You did so much more than you had to for us."

Her full lips called his name. The urge to lean a little closer and pull her into his arms rushed through his mind, and fought with his common sense. What would her kiss taste like? The salty sweetness of the popcorn, or something else. "Thanks Jo. But, I took my life...my privilege for granted."

"Why do you say that?"

"Because it's true." He stood and walked to the window of her office and stared at nothing. "After college, I had plans. None of them included coming back to Memphis. And when I did come back, I guess...I was angry."

"Angry?"

"At the world for not allowing me to succeed on my own terms, without my parents."

"Hating the world is a lot of anger to carry around. I think joining the military was my way of escaping from or dealing with a lot of mine. Why did you give up?"

"I don't think I realized I did." He returned to his seat. "Not until I met you. Woman, you're a fighter."

Her dark skin softly colored with a cinnamon hue. "I don't know if I'm a fighter."

"You are a beautiful inspirational fighter."

"Beautiful inspirational fighter. I think I like that." She leaned nearer, the smell of caramel and salt grabbed onto him. "Are you hitting on me...right here?" She glanced around. "In my office?"

"Hitting on you?" It sounded dumb even to him. "I've hit on a lot of women, but no I'm not hitting on you. I'm being honest. You are the most beautiful woman I've ever seen, and you inspire me. You make me want to be a better man." He sat back and pressed play on the DVD player's remote.

"You make me want to be a better man." The words floated through Jo's mind as she ran through the trails of Shelby Farms with Carmen. Cyclists and in-line skaters buzzed by pulling her away from the words of Whitney that paced her run and her mind. Every inch of the tiny powerhouse beside her pumped with adrenaline. Although she was taller, and had a longer stride, she had to work hard to keep up with the other woman's pace. Maybe compensating for past ills, or maybe because of her military training, the woman worked out every day, and she, like an idiot, tagged along most days. She pulled earphones from her ears, and let them dangle.

"What's going through your head?" Carmen asked.

"I don't know." To be honest, she had no real idea of what to do about the feelings she had for Jeremy. They were nothing alike. Just thinking."

"About what? Or, should I say who?" She smiled.

She stopped running, and dropped her hands to her thighs panting loudly. "God, is it that obvious?" Breath after breath, she dragged in long deep breaths through her mouth, instead of her nose, in an attempt to relax her heart rate. Bugs and whatever else flying through the air caused her to choke.

Carmen grabbed the water bottle from her hip and handed it to her. The freaking woman looked like she could run a marathon if a starter's gun rang out. "Pretty much to everyone." She took the bottle from Jo and took a sip.

"How? I only just admitted the thoughts to myself." Jo marveled as Carmen twisted her body into various contortions to stretch. Meanwhile she found the closest bench, and laid across the warm wood. "I think he's really interested, and I love the way I feel when I'm around him, but we come from completely different worlds."

Carmen stopped stretching. "So what?"

"I met his parents the other day. I felt like his father watched me the entire time. He barely spoke. And his mom. She was like something out of an old movie or something." Something inside of her searched for memories of her childhood. Before that day when her mother packed everything Jo had into a suitcase and drove her to Nashville. "I barely remember my mother, and my dad...nothing, no memories."

"So, what you're saying is that you think you're not good enough because you don't come from the same background or type of family as Jeremy?"

"When you put it that way it doesn't sound good at all." On a sigh, she flung an arm across her eyes. "I don't really have anything. I'm starting over. A few months ago, I was living out of my car."

Carmen lifted Jo's feet, sat, and rested Jo's legs across her thighs. "Is he asking you for anything?"

"No. Not even a date, but I don't know what I'd do if he did."

"Girl, you have a lot to offer to anyone. You're a good person, and you deserve everything you've received." She took another sip from her water bottle. "You should figure that out because I think it'll happen and soon."

"Jo, my daughter is going to meet us for lunch," said Mrs. Hooks. I hope that you don't mind."

Jo shifted around a bit in the passenger's seat to take full advantage of the seat warmer. "No, it's not a problem. Will she be reviewing the sites with us?"

"Oh no. Ms. Velma and I had a great time picking out sites over the past days. We just thought you should choose between the top three. My daughter wanted me to meet her at her caterer's office for a tasting."

"We can finish this later, or I can go out to see the last one alone. I don't want to intrude."

They pulled to the curb and the valet met Mrs. Hooks at her door. Jo had only been to the restaurant once before, but it was one of her favorites. As they entered a whiff of something delicious hit her nose. Molasses. Jo stared at the plate of scallops, and something she couldn't identify as the waiter carried it to a table close by. After checking with the hostess, Jo and Mrs. Hooks were led to a table where a petite blond, whose features perfectly mimicked Jeremy's waited.

At the sight of her mother, she sprang from the table. "Mom, I'm so excited." She began to unfold an envelope and show it to Mrs. Hooks. "Look, aren't they gorgeous!"

After a quick review, Mrs. Hooks agreed. "Beautiful." Then she turned to Jo. "What do you think?"

Jo's mouth hung open for a brief moment. Then she took the thick paper in hand and skimmed her fingers across it. "The paper is so thick and the imprint of your monogram is gorgeous."

The woman beamed at her. Then, she extended her hand. "Thanks! I'm Heather." They shook hands. "You must be Jo." They all sat at the table. "I've heard so much about everything you and the Mitchells are doing at the church."

"And after this fundraiser, we'll be able to do even more," added Mrs. Hooks.

"Thank you both." Jo sipped from the water waiting for her at the table. "But, Mrs. Hooks can you handle helping Heather with her wedding and us with the fundraiser? That's a lot for us to ask."

Mrs. Hooks smiled. "Flo. Call me Flo. And it's fun for me to help you both." She reached out and placed a hand over whichever hand of theirs was closest to her.

"Haven't you heard? My mother is a super woman!" Heather removed all the wedding portfolios that littered the table. "After she found out what kind of need there was and what you guys were struggling with there was no turning back."

"We've been working on Heather's wedding for a year." Flo's eyes lit up as brightly as Heather's at the mention of the wedding. "The day is going to be so magical." Flo stared into the distance as she spoke. "Outdoors at the Botanical Gardens."

"Yes. Everything will be beautiful, not too hot." Heather bounced in her chair. "You should come. You could be Jeremy's date."

"Heather, that's an absolutely wonderful idea," added Flo.

"Uhh," Jo didn't know what to say, "Doesn't Jeremy already have a date?"

"No, and he'd love it!" said Heather.

Jo stared at the two women, amazed. They'd invited her for Jeremy. He'd flirted and she'd flirted back, but that didn't really mean he'd want to take her to his sister's wedding. "Maybe, but I'll wait on his invitation before I buy my dress."

"Heather tells me that I'll be uninvited if you're not my plus one," Jeremy said with a grin as he strolled up to her.

Jo stared at that smile and wondered how many women had been on the receiving end of that same gorgeous little grin. God, she knew there had to have been a lot of them. She, on the other hand, couldn't remember the last time she'd been on a real date. Half of her childhood in foster care, and most of her twenties in the military hadn't allowed her a lot of time for dating, or anything else.

"It looks like you might be uninvited."

His smile disappeared. "What? Why?"

Voices echoing through the halls alerted them to the approach of the women whose arrival they'd been waiting.

"We've worked together, but you haven't taken me on one date." She turned to check the doorway behind her. "Why would I go to something like your sister's wedding with you? Because she threatened you?" She'd love to go with him, but only if he wanted to take her. Not a pity date. Or, because his mother and sister liked her. She wanted him to *want* her.

His pale skin reddened with embarrassment before a sinful little grin turned the corner of one side of his mouth. "You want me to take you on an 'official' date?"

Now, she was the one who felt embarrassed. If the lights in the screening room of the studio were brighter, he'd know it, too. "I don't want a sympathy date."

The expression on his face became more serious than she'd expected. "I don't spend time with you because I feel obligated. Or, out of sympathy or pity. I enjoy spending time with you."

The longer he stared, the more exposed she felt. Their chairs were too close. He gripped her chair, and pulled her nearer. The watery fresh scent of his cologne dragged her in closer. "I didn't mean it in a negative way," she managed to say.

"It doesn't matter. I want to be clear why I spend my time with you."

The voices in the hallway were closer now. "Okay."

"We'll plan a date," he said.

"Okay." For some reason, she'd lost her ability to form longer sentences.

"I'll take you on an 'official' date. But, do you think you can handle it?"

She had no response because she didn't know the answer.

"Handle what?" asked Carmen. Flanked by the other four women, they all waited for a response.

"Nothing," Jo answered. "We were talking about his sister's wedding." Carmen flashed a knowing (although irritating) smile, and then sat. The other women chatted to each other, unaware of the last exchange.

After the women were all in place, Jeremy began the showing. At all of the appropriate places, the women sniffed, sat in complete silence, or cheered.

When it ended, Carmen spoke again. "I know my girlfriend said this already, but Jeremy that was beautiful. I didn't think people cared." She searched the faces of the women around her. "When you're fighting through it you feel alone. When I met these women, I realized I wasn't."

"Thank you, Carmen," he said.

"You didn't make me feel embarrassed when I saw myself on the screen," Carmen added.

"It was nice to see the pictures of what the shelter will look like," added Jessica. "There's going to be a lot of things there for children." She bowed her head a little after speaking. Veronica wrapped an arm around her.

Everyone discussed their favorite parts of the documentary.

"Ladies, I know I dragged you all out kind of late to view this for me. What if I take you all to dinner or maybe dessert," he stated.

The ladies exchanged glances.

"I swear. I'll be on my best behavior." He pointed over his shoulder with a thumb. "There's a pizza place right around the corner."

Carmen stood. "Let's go."

Jeremy helped Jo into her coat. After she pushed her arms through, and she turned to face him, she whispered, "This is not a date."

He smiled as his hands slid down the length of her coat fingering each button until she was all buttoned up. "I thought you might feel safer with chaperones."

Chapter Eight

"Jo, you have a guest at the front desk," said Jazmine, the receptionist at her office.

She wasn't expecting anyone. "I'll be right out." A quick check in the reflection of the framed picture across from her desk, and she headed to the waiting area. *Heather?*

"Hi Jo!" She hugged her. "I hope it's okay I dropped by."

"Sure." She motioned towards the door. "Do you want to go to my office?"

"Well, actually, I was kind of hoping that you could come with me." She did a little shy girl bob and twist of her feet.

"Come with you?"

"Well, mom was supposed to come with me to my fitting, but she's working on something with the fundraiser and is on the other side of town."

"You sure you want my help?"

"Well, mom thought that since my fitting is on this side of town that you could maybe use a break, and come with me. I'd love the company," she pleaded.

"I don't have a lot left for the day, but are you sure you don't want to just wait for your mom or somebody? I don't have any experience picking out wedding dresses." She didn't know anything about anything to do with weddings, birthday parties, anniversaries, or any kind of celebration. Somewhere between foster care and the military, she'd lost sight of the importance of those things.

A shadow of disappointment crossed Heather's face. "I guess...if you don't have time. I'll have more fittings before the wedding. Thanks." She turned to leave.

"Wait. No, I meant this is such a special thing, I don't want to ruin it." She took a long breath. "I don't know a thing about wedding dresses."

Heather grabbed her arm. "Is that all? No problem." She flipped her shoulder-length blonde hair. "Just tell me I'm gorgeous unless, I'm really hideous." She smiled.

"Okay, well, give me a second to grab my purse, and I'll meet you outside."

"Awesome!"

Twenty OH-MY-GOD I'm riding with a crazy person minutes later, she sat with a glass of wine waiting for Heather to appear in her first selection.

Heather stepped through the curtains. "What do you think?" She grabbed the skirting and did a little twirl.

Wine stung that strange little place between the roof of her mouth and her nose. "Uhh."

"You don't like it?" Heather's face slumped.

"It's nice, but it doesn't show your beautiful figure." She sat her wine down and walked towards Heather. Tugging at different spots on the dress, she spoke. "Look at this. I know they could take this in, but you have the smallest waist ever, and this, even after taking it in, won't fit it right."

Heather spun around a bit in the mirror. "You're right." She stepped off the platform, and headed back towards the dressing area. "Next."

Dress after dress, they searched.

This time, Heather stepped out in a vintage lace dress that was gorgeous! "I think this one might be a little frumpy for me."

What? "It's gorgeous, but maybe it's a little 'older' than you'd like." Jo couldn't stop touching the lace of the dress. It was not white, but a slightly off-white beige color. The bodice fit perfectly. Sleeveless. Beautiful.

"You love this one, huh?" asked Heather as she bounced from the platform. "You should definitely wear this one at your wedding." She disappeared behind the curtain.

My Wedding?

Heather sprung through the curtains twirling in circles. The train of this dress wasn't long, but it wasn't short. It gathered around her feet as she spun. Her hands flitted across the rhinestones embedded in silver stitching along the bodice. "It's beautiful. I love it!"

It was. But, more importantly, she glowed in it. "I think you found your prefect dress."

"Alright, sweetie, tell me again."

"Mama Velma, it's not that big of a deal," Jo replied.

"You went wedding dress shopping with Jeremy's sister." She did one of those long slow I know more than you do glances. "Did you like the dresses?"

"Some were awful." She laughed. "But, some were absolutely beautiful." She pictured the beautiful lace dress. "The one Heather really loved was white with rhinestones stitched in silver threading."

"It sounds beautiful." She kept sifting through the donations strewn across the table, quickly tossing them into piles: discard, clean, or keep. "Pastor and I can't wait until your wedding day."

"What?" They'd be waiting for an awfully long time for that one. She was sure.

"You will do it here, in the church." She stopped sorting. "With us?" The older woman's eyes hinted to more questions than answers. She'd been more of a mother to her than her own, who'd given her up because having a daughter became too much for her to handle. But, this woman welcomed her and the mess that was her life into her home and her heart.

Jo hugged her, hard. "Of course." She let go and stepped back. "If it ever happens. But, mama Velma, you know I don't think it ever will."

"Of course it will, child." She sat, and pulled Jo down beside her. "You still believe that you deserve happiness, right?"

Honestly, Jo didn't know what she believed any more. She knew she'd been blessed to walk or hobble into the church that night, but she didn't know what was planned for her. "You and the pastor were a gift I never expected." She bowed her head. "Because of you I wake up every day thankful."

"Sweetie, you've just got to find the courage to love with an open heart." Mama Velma's smile, that had faded earlier, blossomed. God, her smile lightened Jo's heart. "You are one of the strongest women I've ever known." Her hands covered Jo's. "It was no mistake that you were brought into our lives."

"You and pastor always say that."

"We always wanted children, but to give birth to our own wasn't God's plan." Her eyes searched above. "Maybe because he knew you were looking for us."

"Mama Velma, you think there's a master plan for everything."

She stood and began to sort again. "Oh, sweetie, there is. There is." She stood and resumed her sorting tossing a few pieces of clothing around. "Now, tell me more about these wedding dresses."

The sound of someone clearing their throat pulled her from the hypnotic lure of the moon. She turned to find herself staring into Jeremy's gaze. His brown eyes were as mesmerizing as the moon. He spoke, but she didn't hear him. No matter how hard she focused on his mouth, his lips, she couldn't hear a word.

She watched as he sat on the concrete bench beside her. Again, he spoke, this time she heard him. "Jo. Are you okay?"

"Yes. Why?"

"I've been calling your name for awhile."

"Sorry. This place is so beautiful to me."

He looked around the gardens. "It's more beautiful in the summer, but it can get really hot in Memphis in the summer. Spring and early fall are probably the best times to be here."

"How'd you know I was here?"

"I hope I'm not disturbing you, but I dropped by the church on the way home and Mrs. Mitchell told me I could find you here."

"It's my thinking spot." A brisk wind blew through the gardens bending and pushing at the trees and bushes waiting for spring. She bundled a little tighter into the soft warmth of her coat.

He pulled her nearer, and rubbed his hands along the length of her arm. "Are you cold? How long have you been sitting out here?"

"I'm not cold, but I have been here for awhile, we could leave." She stood to walk towards the doors. "Why were you looking for me?"

He pulled her back to the bench beside him. For a moment, he stared into her eyes. In those seconds, she could feel her own breath catch. She wasn't sure of what he would do, but she knew what she wanted him to do. A breeze wrapped around them, and the scent of him mixed with the smells of the gardens. She inhaled deeper and deeper, waiting.

Gently, his lips touched hers. Soft, but firm, his closed lips teased hers. When her lips parted, so did his, and his tongue explored her mouth becoming familiar with her lips and her tongue. The more she responded the deeper and stronger his mouth searched hers. She wrapped her hands around his neck, and held on.

His hands sifted through the strands of her hair as they rotated from her hair to her neck. She hadn't realized how much she craved his touch until now. She allowed herself to fall deeper into his kiss and his touch. It'd been so long since she'd known the touch of a man. Known the passion of a man.

She tore herself away from his embrace. The loss of his touch sent a chill though her body. He stared at her with a question in his eyes. "I'm sorry."

"No, I shouldn't have." He slid down the bench a little. "I shouldn't have jumped you like that."

She reached for his thigh and rubbed a hand along it. Although she tried, she couldn't shut her mind to the hard muscle beneath the fabric of his slacks. She didn't think she'd be able to continue to touch him for long. Each touch made her long for another. And with each, her appetite grew stronger for more than a simple touch or kiss. "You didn't jump me. I wanted you to kiss me."

He slid closer. "Why'd you pull away?"

Her hand fell away from him. "Because it's been a *long* time for me, and you...you're from the advanced class." She smiled. "I'm sure."

"How long is 'long time'?" he asked.

She straightened her back, and stared him in the eye as she said, "Never."

He blinked at her admission. "Never? Never what?"

"I've dated, of course, but I've never been intimate with a man. I don't know if you can or want that. Me."

"You can't be real." His eyes held onto hers and she knew he saw the truth in her words. "I've never met a woman like you before."

Something inside of her began to cry. She was going to lose him before she really had him. He would never want a woman with so many issues, and she was a virgin!

The feel of his hand caressing her cheek released the tears hiding inside.

"Why are you crying?"

"I don't know." She sniffed.

He wiped away each tear. "I don't know why you were brought into my life." His hands fell. "You deserve much better."

"Better?"

"I've had a lot of women..." He continued, "I can't remember the last time I went to church."

She didn't let him finish. Instead, she kissed him. Not passively, but with her heart. She wrapped her arms around his neck, and pulled him close to her. If she didn't, he wouldn't have to run because she might runaway herself.

Jeremy pulled away from her and stood. He took her by the hand and dragged her from the gardens pass the hushed voices and knowing smiles. She didn't care what they'd seen or what they said. She'd needed him to know how she felt. *What she wanted.*

Derailed

At her car, he took her keys and opened her door. She slid into the driver's seat. "Are you coming with me?" she asked.

He reached for her, and tugged her from her seat. Her back rested against the back passenger door. The length of his body pressed into hers. She memorized the feel of each part of him: chest, stomach, and thighs. All of him felt good. She wrapped her arms around his waist, and shoved her hands into his back pockets. The curve of his butt rounded her hands.

Again, he kissed her, softly, before trailing his lips along her chin and neck. Then, he returned his attention to her mouth. Briefly, he suckled her bottom lip before he secured the back of her head with one of his hands. She relaxed her head into his hand, and he drew her in closer and closer. The more they kissed the stronger her body responded. The tension in her breasts and the ache between her legs begged for his touch.

She tore herself from his embrace and stared into his eyes. "Are you coming with me?" she asked again.

An instant soberness overtook him and the haze that covered his eyes when she first glanced into them cleared. He rested his forehead against hers. "Not tonight."

"Why not?"

He kissed her on the cheek. "Because tonight, I'm not ready."

Chapter Nine

Jeremy bumbled around his office, shelving and re-shelving everything he saw.

"Son, what are you doing?"

Sleeves rolled up to his elbows, his producer hovered in the doorway. Neal's premature grey hair and heavily wrinkled brow would mislead anyone looking of his true age. Younger than his father, Neal had graduated a year behind his dad, but he was a member of the same fraternity, and as loyal now to the elder Hooks as he had been when they were young men in college. And now, a relationship that he'd abused, he was quickly beginning to appreciate. Jo hadn't had the benefit of the same kind of relationships and connections to help her. *Shit!* He'd taken a lot for granted.

He fell into the cushions of the couch placed opposite a nearby window. "Nothing." He looked up from his position. "What's up?"

"The documentary is a good piece of work."

"Thanks."

"Would you like to cover the fundraiser for the show?"

"Could we work that in?"

"We could make it fit."

"I think Jo would love that."

"Jo?"

"I meant the Mitchells. The church."

Neal didn't question his correction. He turned and walked away with a smile. He was quickly growing tired of that smile. Everyone had it. His mother, father, Heather, and now Neal.

He picked up the phone to call Jo and tell her the great news. *Please answer.*

"Hello." The sound of her voice reminded him of the taste of her kiss that night in the gardens. Chocolate with a hint of something, maybe pineapple. Delicious.

"Hi."

"I was just thinking of you."

"I hope it was good," he paused. "Tell me."

She laughed. "They weren't *those* kinds of thoughts." Silence. "Why did you leave last night?"

How was he going to explain how much she confused him? "Believe me...I wanted to go with you."

"So. Why didn't you?"

"You are different for me. I don't want to hurt you."

"I'm a big girl. I can take care of myself."

"I know."

"What do you want?"

"A date?"

After a brief silence, she spoke, "I was thinking I don't have a date for the fundraiser or your sister's wedding."

"Will you go with me?"

"Is that it? No romantic gestures of invitations?"

"Should I ask for your hand from the pastor, too?"

"Yep." She laughed. "He'd love that one."

"I will be your date for everything," he stated.

"Everything? That covers a lot."

"Yes, it does." Lately, she'd been the only thought in his head. When he wasn't with her, he was staring at her pictures, or his copy of the documentary. She'd taken over all of him. "I called to tell you my producer is going to let me cover the fundraiser for a piece on the news."

"Jeremy, that's fantastic!" she exclaimed. "The pastor will be so happy. You and your mother have done so much for us."

"Hopefully, the results will be good enough to get the shelter built without loans, or using funds needed for something else." Either would break her heart, and slow the ability for her and the church to accomplish what was needed to help the women in need of the shelter.

"Your mom and Ms. Velma have worked miracles. Every ticket has been sold! Hopefully, we'll receive enough individual donations that we'll blow the top off the little thermostat posted on the wall of the pastor's office." She laughed.

Jeremy stood in the middle of the room surveying his camera layout. After a few run-throughs of the audio system with the team, he searched the room for his date. What kind of date was this? She didn't come with him because he had to ride over with his team, and she arrived early with Ms. Velma, his mother, and sister. He hadn't seen the woman in days, which may have been a good thing because his body reacted to the thought of her. Between the fundraiser and his sister's wedding, his family had taken over and there didn't seem to be much he could do about it.

No sign of Jo, but his father and Pastor Mitchell sat nearby heavily involved in a discussion that blinded them to his approach. "Pop, pastor have you seen Jo?"

They fell back into easy laughter. "You'll never find her. Not until the event is over," said the pastor. "This is all she and my wife have talked about for weeks."

His father spoke. "Son, this is their night. Next to your sister's wedding your mother hasn't had this much fun in years."

Stern faced, the pastor said, "My wife, I'm afraid, is secretly planning a wedding." The pastor stared at Jeremy as he finished his statement. Then he broke into laughter again. Jeremy's dad joined in.

"Pastor?"

"It's okay, son." The pastor and his father laughed harder. "I told her you young people haven't been dating for long."

His father added, "Not many months at all." He gestured at a seat beside them for Jeremy to sit. "But, the short time Jo has been in your life has created a difference in you that your mother and I noticed." His father studied him. "I'm sorry son for not believing in you...not allowing you to be your own man, your own way."

"It's alright. I know you wanted me to be a different kind of man." A man he tried to be, but was sure he didn't want to be. He knew the man he wanted to be, and Jo had inspired him to take a chance on being him.

His father reached out and placed a hand on his shoulder. As a boy, his father's grip had been as strong and firm as you'd expect of a man his size. He easily had Jeremy by an inch, but tonight, his hand felt as light as a feather on his shoulder. "No...not different. I wanted you to be the man I knew you could be." He seemed to search for words. "You are your own man. When you told your mom and me of your love for photography, I didn't think it was a man's way to make money and provide for a family. I'm sorry that was the way my father had taught me."

The pastor contributed, "We all have our views of what a man's role in a family should be." He scanned his eyes across the staff preparing the room for the evening's event. "Believe it or not my grandfather didn't think women should work outside of the home. '...take care of the children...' is what women were supposed to do." He laughed. "Could you imagine what he'd think of my Jo?" He sipped from his tea. "I can't imagine her not being exactly who she is. Doing exactly what she's doing." He held up a hand and measured out an inch with his thumb and forefinger. "But, I'd love to see her slow down a little bit." On a deep sigh, he leaned back in his chair. "That's what we old folks do when it comes to the children we love."

"Exactly pastor." His father cleared his throat. "I tried to force my opinions on you, and that almost lost me my only son." He picked up a copy of the coffee table book Jeremy put together to support the documentary as part of the fundraising program. "These pictures are powerful. The people who come tonight will dig a little deeper because of this." He shook the book. "Your work will make an impact. I'm proud of the man that you are son."

Jeremy had never heard those words from his father before. He stared into the eyes of his father unlike his own, they were blue. According to his mother "...the most beautiful blue eyes." His father's words gave him the confidence he needed to say what he wanted to say next, though it took him a moment to find his voice. "I love you and mom. I walked around for a long time, not really understanding. Now, I do." He turned to the pastor. "The last few months have taught me more than the last years combined. I have a long way to go, but..." He focused his attention on the pastor. "Pastor, I don't want to do it alone."

Derailed

The pastor's smile widened. "Well, young man, I think you're about to make my wife the happiest woman. Then again, maybe, my Jo will be happier." He laughed.

Jo stepped out onto the stage. This time it was a stage, not raised platforms, or the dais of the church, where she was incredibly comfortable. From where she stood, behind a huge podium, she couldn't make out one face. She searched for anything to let her know where Jeremy, or the pastor and mama Velma might be in the audience. She knew where their table (her table) was located, but couldn't make out a thing.

The words she'd rehearsed jumbled in her head. Crap! She froze. She'd been alone for most of her life. Standing in the dark with a spotlight aimed at her, she should be able to handle it. But instead, blank, she stared into the audience. Center the room, in the rear, the camera began to swing a little. Not much, but the side to side motion of the light let her know the camera swung, softly. *Jeremy.* She smiled and the words began to rush back to her mind, and she spoke.

At the conclusion of her speech, for a brief moment, the lights in the hall were raised as the stage was set for the presentation of Jeremy's documentary. In those seconds, she saw him, in the back, his smile shot across the room at her. Or, maybe, she imagined it. But, either way, it warmed her heart and her body. She floated down the stairs to the table where her family and his sat waiting. The smiles and calming voices at the table comforted her.

Even though she'd seen the documentary several times, its delicacy with the treatment of the women and their situations touched her heart. Jeremy could've done anything. He could've shown the women as junkies, dirty, or the children as lacking and not focused the film on causes and resolutions. But, that's exactly what he did. He showed their flaws, but he highlighted why and what could be done to help them. She didn't know he'd managed to take the time to visit one of the larger centers in Houston, and had inserted a few interviews she hadn't seen. This remarkable man had done all of it to help the church. To help her.

After the pastor and Mrs. Mitchell gave the closing remarks for the evening, they all poured over the tallies to check and double check their numbers.

Everyone picked through the receipts and the numbers in front of them. No one spoke.

"I'm so sorry. I thought we'd hit our goal," said Mrs. Hooks.

"This was a great night," announced the pastor. "We may not have received all the donations we were in need of, but this night has made our journey shorter, and grown our family." He hugged his wife around the shoulders. "What do you think, Mrs. Mitchell?" He smiled.

She walked from him to where Jo stood, and sifted her fingers through Jo's new short cropped bob before she cupped the sides of Jo's face in her hands. "I think our Jo shined. And with the donations we received, we're going to be able to raise the rest of the money in no time at all." The smaller woman's eyes danced with a joy Jo couldn't explain.

Different voices joined in chorus agreeing with mama Velma's sentiments.

Jo was thankful for their graciousness, but she had to admit, she'd be much happier if they would've hit the *magic* number. She hadn't seen any expressions of sadness or disappointment on the faces of the women, her friends, featured in the documentary. Carmen had gone as far as mentioning how the Hooks family had really jumped in and "became a part of the team."

On the ride back to her place, Jo didn't have much to say. Jeremy had done so much to help her. The photo book and the documentary. His mother and mama Velma had found the location, even though they "allowed" her to make the final decision. But, what had she really done. "Did I let you guys down?" she asked.

"Let us down?" Jeremy responded.

"We didn't fall short by much, maybe I missed something." She sank into the car seat as she finished her statement.

He reached out an arm and stroked the back of her head. His touch was beginning to wear down the little resolve she had left. After years of pushing people away, now, she welcomed him. Without thinking, she grabbed his hand and kissed his palm. The touch of his hand to her mouth gave her a comfort that she'd never known.

"Baby, there was nothing you could've done." He pulled into the underground parking garage of her building. "We all did our best. We'll have to find another way to raise the rest of what's needed."

"We?"

"Of course, we're in this together." They sat in the quiet lot while he continued. "You're not alone, anymore. You don't have to do it by yourself."

The touch of his lips to hers set off little flutters that scared her as much as it excited her. The kiss ended as abruptly as it began, and instantly his warmth was missed.

They exited the car and walked to her apartment in silence. Inside, she asked, "Can you stay tonight?"

Chapter Ten

Her request slammed into his chest. He surveyed the silver dress hugging the innocent enticing curves of her body, right down to the nude stockings covering her long legs that ended at those damn rose red shoes. He imagined the feel of the stocking against his finger tips, his lips. Tonight, he should say no. "Yes."

With her curled up in his arms on the couch, he understood why his father and the pastor were happy. If it's the right woman, it doesn't matter what you're doing, it's the *right* thing. As she napped, he dragged his hand along the length of her body causing his own pain. He stared at the television for some sort of divine intervention to quiet the ache growing stronger. It begged him for something he couldn't do. He eased her head to a nearby pillow. He needed to run to a shower or somewhere and cool off. But, she woke. Her heavy hooded eyes spoke to him before her words.

"Where are you going?" she whispered.

"I wanted something to drink."

"Oh." She yawned. "I'd love some hot tea." She stood and stretched the length of her body. She wasn't trying to drive him crazy, but she did it well. "I'll get it." She tugged him back to the couch. "Sit."

He leaned across the arm of the couch, and watched. Barefoot. Bare legged. She strolled into the kitchen with that silver dress, riding up her thighs, drawing his attention to all the parts of her body he'd like to explore. She had to know that dress would capture the attention of any man watching.

She balanced two cups of hot tea and honey as she returned to him. Locked on the sway of her hips, when she stopped moving something inside of him wanted him to think of a reason to send her back to the kitchen so that he could watch it all over again. But, instead, he took the tea and drank a long sip. A shot of brandy in the tea would have calmed him more.

After falling to the cushion beside him, she leaned back against the arm of the couch and tossed her legs across his thighs. Auto-drive kicked in and his hand slid up her thigh to the hem of her dress. *Stop! Not yet.* He looked up to find her staring at him as hard as he stared at the legs that disappeared underneath the hem of that dress. "I'm sorry."

"Me, too." She shifted and dropped her legs to the floor. "Is there something wrong with me?"

What? "No." He slid closer. "I...just have a plan for us." He pondered his words. "I don't want this to be a short thing." He reached out, and placed a hand below her chin to raise her eyes to his. "I've fallen in love with you, Jo," he waited. "I want you to be okay with everything that happens between us."

"I am." She kissed him. "I'm okay with everything," She placed her cup of tea on the floor, and took his from his hand and placed it beside hers. Then, she wrapped her arms around his neck, and pulled him into a deeper kiss. Not tender like the first one, but filled with nervous passion. She hesitated when his hands slid from her hips along her torso to rest beside her breasts.

He reached around and unclasped her hands from his neck. "Baby, I won't be able to say no to you all night." He sat back. "I only want you, but not just for tonight...for always."

"Always," she repeated with a wide-eyed stare.

The ring he wanted to give her had been a part of his family for generations. Proposing without a ring might be stupid. "I spoke to the pastor." Her smile widened. "He gave me his blessing, and so did Ms. Velma." He dropped to one knee. "It's strange...before I met you...I knew something was missing, but I wasn't sure what." He didn't have a ring to slide on her finger. Instead, he kissed where it should be placed. "Now, I know I was living, but not really living." He caressed her finger. "I am a better man than I was when you met me. I will be a good husband, father, friend...whatever you need." The words rushed through his mind. "I know I don't have a ring, but I promise. I have one." He smiled. "Will you marry me?"

Just five months ago, she sat on the cold ground with nothing. But, after one sleep-deprived night, she found a family who loved her, and a man who thinks she's worth his love. A man who wants to marry her. She held her hand in the air, and imagined the ring. She knew it would beautiful, but its sparkle wouldn't compare to the glow in the eyes of the man before her. What would it be like to be his wife? The mother of his children? "For so long, I tried to hold the pieces of my life together. The tighter I held onto what I had, the harder and harder it became." Tears fell. "I've been afraid for so long. Afraid that I'd never meet anyone like you." She slipped her hands from his, and cradled his head in her hands. "I've been waiting on you for a long time." She exhaled a heavy breath. "Yes." She couldn't manage much more. "I love you."

He rose from his knees. Her body tingled with anticipation. She craved his touch in ways that she'd never craved any man's touch.

Strong and determined, his hands slid up her thighs. This time they didn't stop, but, instead, he pushed her skirt up with his hands and they traveled higher. She closed her eyes, leaned back into the cushions behind her and waited. But, nothing.

He hovered above her. "I want you." His hands slid along her waist. "But, I've never had to wait for much. I know you're worth the wait."

"But..." *I've waited so long.*

"I will be the first man and the only man you'll know," he paused. "I want that to be on our wedding night."

She wrapped her arms around his neck, and kissed with all the desire she had. "Please." She rubbed her body against his. He couldn't hide his reaction. His body pressed into hers, hard and stiff. His breathing became more erratic. More and more, she pulled his body into hers and wrapped one long leg around his thigh locking his body to hers.

"Are you going to keep doing that?" he asked.

"Is it working?" She knew from the strained look on his face it was, and well.

"What you're doing isn't fair, and if this were any other night."

"What?"

"This would end completely differently, but tonight..." He stood and adjusted his pants. "I'm sleeping on the couch, and you..." He scooped her from where she lay. "...are sleeping in your bed."

"No." She struggled.

He dropped her to her bed. "Yes." He shut the door behind himself.

Epilogue

The music cued and Jeremy and the seated guests turned their attention to the large French doors at the end of the gardens. They were opened and she glided through. The hair that normally flowed freely was pinned and curled precisely to withstand the spring winds of Memphis. But, the dress, it bent and swayed to every wish of the invisible dictator.

Long, sexy legs strolled down the aisle towards him with no hesitation or tremble. As she neared, the floral scent of her bouquet mingled with her perfume calling to him to close the gap between them. Jo took her place. She looked at him, and gave him a wink that calmed his nerves. He couldn't wait until this day was over, and he had her all to himself.

They both turned and waited. His baby sister was beautiful. A tiara and a veil, which skewed her face, slightly, held her hair tightly. But, it could never hide her beauty. She took her place beside her fiancé and with trembling hands passed her bouquet to Jo.

His baby sister was getting married.

The bubbles of Jo's champagne tickled her nose. Hand-in-hand with Jeremy, they chatted up the crowd as they'd been instructed. Jo had never attended anything so lavish. The gardens were always manicured and well-kept, but tonight they were even more beautiful. The water fountains throughout the grounds were glowing with lights and had been filled with beautiful purple flowers. With the additions of the white tents and lighting, the affect of a fairy tale wedding couldn't be denied. She searched for the pastor and mama Velma. They sat with Flo and Milton beaming at everything around them. When she and Jeremy approached, they sprang from the table to hug them.

"Oh, sweetie, you look so beautiful," said Ms. Velma. "Be sure to stand in the back, so that you can catch the bouquet," she whispered with a knowing wink.

She laughed. "Mama Velma..." She pointed at her ring. "I've already got it."

"A little luck never hurts," said mama Velma.

After they'd all made rounds, she sat at the table with Jeremy enchanted by the night, the music, and the man.

Heather and her new husband, Ron, along with Flo and Milton, and *her* parents appeared in front of them with smiles that stretched from ear to ear.

"We have a surprise for you," Jeremy whispered a little too close to her ear. The scent of his cologne intoxicated her.

She fought the desire to snuggle in a little closer and inhale. When she finally glanced into his eyes, he stared at her as if he knew her thoughts. "Surprise?"

"Yeah, if you could tear yourself away from my brother for a minute," Heather quipped. Then, she handed her an envelope. "Ron and I decided we're the kind of the people who have everything we need. So, we asked our guests to donate instead of buying us gifts."

"Open it, Jo," said the pastor.

Confused, she studied the faces of everyone around her. "Heather, Ron...what did you guys do?" She ripped a corner of the envelope and pulled the paper from inside. Her hands went to her face covering her eyes. The tears that welled behind her closed eyes couldn't be restrained. The feel of Jeremy's hand rubbing her back before pulling her near calmed her. "Pastor, this is enough money to finish the shelter!" She jumped from Jeremy's arms to the pastor's.

"Heather, Ron. Thank you!" She hugged them. "You didn't have to...why did you do this?"

"Because we're family," Heather responded. Her eyes glanced around the people standing. "I suggested it to Jeremy, but he thought you wouldn't let us do it. So, I talked it over with mom and dad, and we decided to do it without telling you." She walked to the pastor and mama Velma. "I didn't tell them what I had planned until the rehearsal dinner, yesterday." She clamped her hands together and placed them against her chin. "So, don't be mad at them."

"I'm not mad, but I hate that this took from you."

"I wanted to do it," Heather hugged her. "It's something you believe in, and I believe in you." She stepped back. "This is what sisters do...right, help each other out."

Sisters. She squeezed Heather. "That's what sisters do." Jo walked over and draped her arms around the pastor and mama Velma. "I've always wanted a family. She kissed each on the cheek. Then, walked to Flo and Milton and kissed them before she did the same to Ron and Heather.

She returned to her seat beside Jeremy. "I dreamed of all of you for so long." Tears she'd held back for too many years flowed washing away loneliness, pain, and emptiness that she'd grown so used to that she barely noticed the weight of it until they started chipping it away. I thought I'd be alone forever. I was prepared for it." Softly, she kissed Jeremy again. "But, I'd dreamed...I'd hoped that you'd be here." She couldn't resist the urge to snuggle a little closer. "I hoped with all my heart."

"What would I have done if you'd never returned?" he asked. My life would've been different. I would've been different."

"We don't have to worry about that." She kissed him again. "I'm finally home."

More Great Books from Angela Kay Austin

Give Me Everything

He'd sat on top of the world... the perfect woman, a daughter, and a job that made his father proud. Now, Kendis was divorced, and his daughter wasn't really his. She'd been through the wringer in her personal life, and now LaKia thinks the only thing she can control is her career. Until Kendis. He gave her everything, and she gave it right back.

Sweet Victory

For her employees' sakes, Victoria James quits her job to save theirs and loses the man she thought she loved. Back to Memphis, Tennessee to a forgotten relationship with her grandfather, where everything she has is stolen. Chad Kirkpatrick, her childhood love, the first man to break her heart, now a police officer, comes to her aid. Will she put her past behind her? Will Chad forgive her?

Angela Kay Austin

Bestselling author Angela Kay Austin has expressed herself through words for as long as she can remember. Poems became songs performed with her cousin at every family gathering. But, eventually, short stories filled her favorite pink diary. An infatuation with music and theater led to years playing various instruments and small extra roles in TV shows before giving way to a degree and career in radio and TV production. After completing another degree in marketing, Angela found herself combining her love for all things creative and worked for many many years in promotions and advertising. But once again, she found herself writing, which led to her first published work which stayed on her publisher's bestseller list for ten weeks. Her second release hit the bestseller list at All Romance eBooks.

She's spoken on author panels, and served on boards for various author groups. When she's not writing, you can find her reading her favorite authors, or researching her next story idea. Angela shares her downtime with her mixed-bred rescue terrier—Midnight, in the beautiful southern state of Tennessee.

She's also a member of Romance Writers of America, From the Heart Romance Writers, Chick Lit Writers of the World, and Washington DC Romance Writers.

www.ingramcontent.com/pod-product-compliance
Lightning Source LLC
Chambersburg PA
CBHW060618130626
46555CB00002B/556